Mulling It Over

Mulling It Over

an anthology

Edited by Debz Hobbs-Wyatt and Gill James

Bridge House

British Library Cataloguing in Publication Data

A Record of this Publication is available from the British
Library

ISBN 978-1-907335-93-8

This edition published 2020 by Bridge House Publishing
Manchester, England

Contents

Introduction

Well, we've certainly been given a lot to mull over this year. So this collection has acquired an appropriate title for 2020.

As ever, the interpretation has been varied: the Island of Mull, thinking about things, often quite deeply, the odd mulled drink and even something used in making a book – how appropriate again.

For the first time we received entries anonymously. We were delighted when, once writers' names were revealed, we had elected to publish some authors well known to us. We are also delighted to welcome newcomers.

Our authors have again been a great pleasure to work with.

You will find a variety of styles here and an intriguing mix of voices.

There is humour and pathos, some hard-hitting tales and some feel-good accounts. All to be mulled over.

It's that time of year again: story time. Enjoy!

According to Apes

Dianne Stadhams

"Time to mull it over, macaques-chan," Shiza decreed.

Snowflakes twirled, pine needles twitched and the moon hung low in the heavens. The night would be long. This decision required complex deliberations. The evidence presented issues encompassing ethics and culture. It was serious monkey business.

Miza, Miki and Maza nodded their furry heads in unison, bowed low to each other before scampering to their respective boughs above the steaming waters to consider the conundrum.

What is the right thing to do when the wrong thing is done for the right reasons?

The Japanese macaques, Miza, Miki, Maza and their mate Shiza had been friends for as long as they could recall. Shiza was not as famous as the other three but was, none the less, always included in grand deliberations and all parties. No Shiza, no shenanigans they all agreed. So when Shiza asked the essential question the other three were more cautious with their replies. Of course Shiza always asked the essential question – for him, doing was more important than thinking about action.

"What shall we do? A crime has been committed. We must, in all conscience, act now,' Shiza said.

"I didn't exactly *hear* the crime," muttered Miza.

"I didn't exactly *see* the crime," whispered Miki.

"I didn't exactly *speak* to any evil doers directly," spluttered Maza.

"That's the bog standard reply you always give... hear no, see no, speak no. So clichéd! Heard the one about brass monkeys?" shouted Shiza.

"There's no need to be coarse," they chanted in unison.

8

"I want us to do something," said Shiza.

"Well first you must hear the facts," Miza said.

"Secondly, you must know all the players," said Miki.

"Only then can you give a fair answer on what has happened to who and why," explained Maza. "Those gaigin[1] have wise words that advise all it takes for evil to triumph is for good men to look the other way."

"Humph and hittigans... you'll be praising organ grinders next! Never mind the foreigners, give me the facts in sequence," said Shiza.

And so three, little, Japanese macaques, global stars with their collective proverb, told the tale of the tripod-legged, Netherland, dwarf rabbit and the stolen kumquat.

"Shall I start?" asked Miza.

"Don't you always?" replied Shiza with a shrug.

The three little monkeys shook their head as if to say, "so harsh!"

Shiza took note, zipped his monkey mouth and sat back to listen.

"Konijn-san," began Miza, "was a rabbit, of the dwarf kind, from that low-lying country in Europe famous for... err..."

"Cheese and clogs," suggested Maza.

"Really?" asked Shiza.

"Who cares about clogs?" Miki replied scratching his armpit. "Keep up and get on with the story. We're not trying for literary fiction here. Keep to the facts."

Chastened, Miza continued, "Unfortunately the rabbit had only three legs. It was born that way. Not an auspicious start in life we can agree."

All the monkeys nodded. They were known for being clever and quick-witted, enthusiastic and innovative.

---

[1] Japanese term for foreigners.

Whereas rabbits were rather quiet and scholarly... a bit boring by monkey standards.

"Konijn-san led a sad and lonely life. To be different meant to be shunned. No one wanted to hop around with a tripod rabbit."

The monkeys nodded again. Too true for macaques as well. In their world the biggest monkey thumped the smaller ones. Showing respect to the boss was THE rule. Survival was dependent upon subservience... unless you were famous of course. That gave you some freedom to be cheeky and ignore the boss... some of the time at least. Miza, Miki, Maza and their mate Shiza hung around together as much as possible. Numbers gave clout. They didn't need to thump... often... to maintain their status quo as international known-abouts... even if it was minor league. It was enough to whisper into another macaque ear, "Do that again banana brain and we'll turn into your worst nightmare of a monkey's uncle." However, they found the odd thump also went down well... as a reminder. But hey... that's what monkeys do.

Crippled Konijn-san was very hungry. Carrots, yellow vegetables and greens in general were in short supply. No invitations to rabbit rendezvous were forthcoming thus there was no hope of sustenance. Drastic measures were needed. What options does a rabbit have in these circumstances? Self-reflection on evil ways was not a consideration. Theft was a blinding glimpse of the obvious.

With his tummy rumbling, Konijn-san dreamed of orange trees, lots of them, laden with large fruits dangling ready for him to pluck, peel and stuff into his mouth. He imagined the juice running down his fluffy, white face, the exquisite stickiness that he could re-visit and lick for hours after. Except he was in the Jigokudani Valley. Not one orange tree had ever grown here. And as he lay exhausted and delirious... a pot containing a small tree blooming with orange kumquats… like a mirage to a thirsty gaigin… rose before his tiny rabbit eyes.

"Yes," he said to the stars above, "I may not be in the Sahara but…"

And up he hopped and headed to downtown Nagano station. There he found the traditional, earthenware bowl that he remembered from days past. It housed a bonsai kumquat… in full bloom… thirteen perfect, orange fruits. Konijn-san would live. He was tempted to eat the lot, there and then. But rabbits are well regarded for their innate gentleness and honesty. So despite temptation, he decided to take ten and leave three. He gobbled three straight away, not bothering to peel them. He could have cried with joy… the texture, the tartness, the succulence. Not only did he have food, it was his favourite colour – orange, uplifting and rejuvenating. All would be well in his world.

The quandary was how to transport the other seven for a solo midnight feast. Konijn-san decided to hide them temporarily behind the bowl whilst he searched for something suitable in which to wrap his stash. He placed them carefully out of sight but before he could begin his search for an abandoned paper packet or discarded newspaper, a three-legged crow surprised him.

Rabbits and crows are not naturally friends. And Konijn-san had never, ever seen a crow with three legs before except on the T-shirts worn by the Japanese national soccer team during their recent visit to the hot springs. He wasn't sure whether to growl or run. In the interests of kumquats and banquets, he affected a bravado he did not feel and thumped his single, hind leg.

"Stone the crows, what have we here, a bunny minus a limb? You born that way Bobtail or have a run in with a train?"

Affronted by the bird's bluntness, he replied softly, "My name is Konijn-san."

11

The bird was not impressed.

"I'm the son of the great Yata-garasu. You must have heard of him?"

Konijn-san shook his head.

"That's the trouble with the youth of today. Know nothing about the history of our illustrious past. I blame the parents and the teachers and the politicians and the…"

"I'm sure you're correct," Konijn-san agreed, worried that his stash might be discovered by this garrulous bird brain, "but I am just passing by to collect my take-away dinner."

"You planning to eat all those kumquats yourself? I saw you stuff three already. Ever thought of sharing with a feathered friend?"

"I'm very hungry," said Konijn-san, his ears twitching in pleasure at the F word. Never before had any living creature suggested they would be his friend. What should he do? His front paw trembled with excitement as he contemplated his next move.

The bird look bored.

"Perhaps I could give you one? We rabbits are kind and generous when we can be."

"My need is greater than yours," said the bird.

"How long since you have eaten?" asked Konijn-san. Food was precious but so was an offer of friendship.

"What's that got to do with the price of rice?"

"I'm very, very hungry. I haven't eaten for many moons," replied Konijn-san.

"I'm not planning to eat those orange bits. I'm going to trade them and do something good with the proceeds. So my need is nobler than your greed."

"Theft for selfish gain?" asked Konijn-san, unsure of the bird's motive.

"My grandmother, who is very, very old, needs my help. That is not being selfish. I plan to exchange the fruit for an old kimono. The silk is so very soft. For an old bird like my esteemed grandmother it will provide a very comfortable and warm lining for her nest… for the rest of her days."

Konijn-san could not argue with that. Yata-garasu was a learned son of a famous elder who was trying to help someone frailer than a hungry, tripod rabbit like himself. In any case he didn't want to fight a big bird with a very pointed beak. Such a pursuit would not end well… for a rabbit. He offered the spoils to the bird, with a deep bow.

Yata-garasu couldn't believe his good fortune. He thought he might have to wrestle the fruits from the odd looking rabbit. Such a strategy would not end well… for a bird… because bird lore warned of rabbits with their big teeth and mean right jabs.

As the bird flew off he couldn't help but be moved by the creature's generosity. Not wanting to display any sentimentality he winked and dropped two of the kumquat cargo back to Konijn-san. The rabbit saluted. The bird dipped a wing. Realpolitik in action… a result for both.

Konijn-san hopped away juggling the fruit between his three legs. It was not easy and sometime between there and home one rolled away. The rabbit did not want to stop and search in the dark. Too many predators might be lurking. And there was one thing tastier than hot bunny and that was hot bob tail in a piquant fruit sauce. He gave a silent wish that whoever found the lone kumquat would use it wisely.

"That's the story," finished Miza.

"They're the players," agreed Miki.

"And you, Shiza, are the macaque amongst us who collected the kumquat," said Maza.

"I didn't steal it," argued Shiza, "I found it. I *did* no evil."

"Nor did I *hear* any evil… in the first animal, so to speak," added Miza.

"Speaking is my prerogative," said Maza. "I didn't hear any of the players *speak* any evil."

13

"And none of us saw any evil, did we?" asked Miki.

Nevertheless four macaques had to consider what is the right thing to do when the wrong thing is done for the right reasons. Saro Kuso[2] they termed it. After some hours, the mystic monkeys re-convened. Consensus was reached. The gravity of the decision was acknowledged.

"A rabbit's got to do what a rabbit's got to do," Miza pronounced.

"Just like a macaque. Konijn-san used the kumquat to save his life," said Miki.

"The bird bargained with the rabbit for a higher cause," added Maza, "no crime in that."

"Finders keepers in my case. No case of evil to be answered," Shiza said.

"Saro Kuso!" they chorused and high-fived their furry paws.

"On that decree I suggest we adjourn to the hot springs to relax," said Shiza. "Snow monkeys we are. Mulled sake wine we have… made with one kumquat, whose provenance is accounted for. No further evidence submitted, case closed. You never monkey with the truth. Kampai tomodachi[3]!"

About the author

Dr Dianne Stadhams has had two plays developed with Bristol Old Vic, two novels shortlisted for global competitions and a young adult novel accepted for publication. In July 2020 she was to be artistic director and writer of a community play in Cornwall, involving over 300 players, entitled *Home Stone…* until Covid-19 derailed the project. In development are a third novel, an illustrated volume of haiku, a film and *Home Stone 2021*. A collection of illustrated short stories, *Links,* is available through Amazon. For further information: www.stadhams.com.

---

[2] Japanese: Saro = Ape, Kuso = Shit
[3] Cheers friends in Japanese.

An Angel at Our Table

S. Nadja Zajdman

Aunt Felicia was a sour woman. The only person she showed affection for was my little brother Mikey. It unnerved him. "What's wrong with me?" Mikey would wail. "She likes me! She doesn't like anybody but she likes me! What's wrong with me?!" I suspect it went against my aunt's principles to demonstrate her true feelings for her own little brother. As a boy, my dad was a prankster. As a man, he donned the cap of the court jester. Yet each Passover it was Daddy who led the Seder service, even though it was held in his brother-in-law's house.

Although raised to become a rabbi, Daddy turned to socialist rebellion. He could recite the Haggadah backwards, forwards, with full expression, and at any speed he chose. One year, Auntie informed my male cousins that they could be excused from the table to watch the hockey play-offs if the service ended before the game did. Hockey play-off games go on forever – but the Seder service goes on longer. Auntie's mistake was to make this promise within earshot of my father.

At first, the shift in rhythm was imperceptible. Daddy began chanting more quickly than usual, and the uncles dutifully picked up the pace. Incrementally, his chanting grew faster and louder and faster still, until he was hurtling through the Haggadah at the tongue-twisting pace of a Danny Kaye patter song. Daddy kept his head down, his face straight, and his eyes fixed firmly on the Hebrew text before him. The uncles were forced to follow as best they could. Auntie fumed in helpless fury. The boys beamed. Before the evening ended, they got to see the last part of the hockey play-off game.

It is the role of the youngest child to open the door for Elijah, prophet, angel, and protector of children, so he can enter the household and drink from the goblet of wine which has been prepared for him. By rights that task should've been performed by my little brother, but when the moment comes for the participants to dip their pinkies into their wineglasses ten times to symbolize the ten plagues which have befallen Egypt – and it comes before the entrance of the angel – Mikey would cuddle up to Mum and merrily dip his pinkie into her wineglass along with her. Whereas Mum would then wipe the residue onto a napkin, like the rest of the grown-ups, Mikey would remove the wine from his finger by licking it off. Ten drops of Manieschewitz was enough to knock him out, and he'd spend the rest of a very long evening curled up on Mum's lap, his pudgy palms clasped as if in prayer and pressed against a cheek, his *yarmulke* askew on his flaxen crew cut, a beatific beam on his cherubic face. Thus, the role of gatekeeper fell to me. "You mean to tell me that he comes to our house and to everybody else's house all at the same time?" I'd ask my dad, when instructed to stand watch.

"Well he's an angel, he can do that. Except in Israel. In Israel he gets there seven hours later, because of the time change."

As my aunts and uncles and older cousins remained at the long dining table continuing the recitation, I was told when to open the door; I was informed when Elijah had finished his drink, and then I was directed to close the front door to my aunt's duplex because Elijah had just made his exit.

"But I can't see the angel!"

"Look harder," urged my father. I squinted. "I still can't see the angel!"

Daddy smiled his warm, gentle smile. "*Shepsaleh*, you have to look with different eyes."

16

My big cousins snickered. The entire tribe insisted they could see Elijah clearly. Surely if I joined my relatives at the table, I'd be able to see the angel too.

"Why can't I just come back to the table and watch the angel drink the wine? Why can't he let himself out?"

"It's not polite to let a guest leave alone. With an angel, you have to be a gentleman."

I had no answer. Yet.

By the time I was eight, I was fed up with this game. "I don't care if I'm a gentleman or not! After I open the door I'm coming back to the table! I want to see him drink!" I was adamant. Daddy quickly improvised. "OK. You can come to the table and you will see the angel drink." (Mikey still couldn't hold his liquor.) When cued, I opened the door for Elijah, as I did every year. I marched back to my aunt's dining room table. Maybe I walked behind Elijah, maybe alongside him. If I bumped into the angel, I didn't notice.

I stood among the adults in front of my aunt's long dining room table which held a large, ornate silver drinking vessel filled to the brim with a deep burgundy-coloured wine. The moment of truth had arrived. "OK." Daddy instructed. "Watch. The angel's going to drink." I held my breath. Daddy slipped his knee under the table and shook it. The silver vessel shimmered under the twinkling crystals of a chandelier. Within the confines of the oval-shaped cup, the dark liquid trembled. I lowered my head and peered. "It didn't go down!" I scowled. "When you drink there's supposed to be less in the glass! It didn't go down!"

My father's frustration was beginning to match my own. He pursed his lips, and pointed to the goblet. "Watch again. The angel's going to drink again!" This time, Daddy kneed the bottom of the table with such force that the wine spilled over the rim and onto the tablecloth – onto my aunt's snow-white tablecloth with the lace trim which she displayed only on special occasions. Auntie stared in horror at the deep burgundy stain.

I gazed at the goblet in wonder and awe. "Oh!" I gleefully clapped my hands, convinced, at long last. "What a sloppy angel!" Daddy was satisfied. Auntie sat stewing over the ruin of her finest linen. She glowered at her youngest brother. Daddy met her smouldering glare and softly, sweetly, in English, he reminded her, "You can't get mad at an angel."

About the author

S. Nadja Zajdman is a Canadian author. Her first short story collection, *Bent Branches,* was published in 2012. Zajdman has had her non-fiction, as well as her fiction, published in newspapers, magazines, literary journals and anthologies across North America, in the U.K., Australia and New Zealand. Zajdman has completed a second work of fiction as well as a memoir of her mother, the pioneering Holocaust educator and activist Renata Skotnicka-Zajdman, who passed away near the end of 2013.

Double Dilemma

Linda W Payne

"Will you take this and give it to Vivienne please? She will find it funny."

My Great Aunt Gillian handed a 1980's Dictaphone to me.

"We used to be audio-typists before the company closed. When they were getting rid of everything I asked if I could have this together with a transcript machine because I thought it may have come in useful." She paused. "But it never did."

Noticing my bemused face at the antiquated machine she smiled. "Well before your day. Come here and I'll demonstrate. The person doing the dictating talks into this machine. See, it has small cassette tapes. Then they hand the tapes to the audio-typist and she types as the tape plays."

I smiled. I could see she was enjoying the memory.

"Mind, we all touch-typed then. Anyway, this one wasn't wiped clean and it was Barry Pearce's once. Vivienne will remember him I'm sure. We all dreaded being given his tapes."

Vivienne is my Gran. Sadly, she is now in a home for people with dementia so anything that triggers a memory can be useful.

"Of course, but you could take it to her yourself."

She looked at her mobility scooter. "I don't think so, luv."

I hugged her and nodded understanding and shoved the museum piece in my handbag.

"Be careful of the record button. It's a toggle switch. Press it to start recording then press again for finish. Like me it's getting old and sensitive." She laughed.

"I'll look after it," I promised. "I must be leaving now Aunt. I want to catch the train before the rush hour begins."

On the near empty train I took my phone from my handbag so I could listen to music. The earphone cable was tangled up inside. "Damn the earplugs." I said as I yanked them out.

As I did so the Dictaphone fell onto the vacant seat beside me. I picked it up intending to put it in my bag but was too absorbed in scrolling down my phone to notice I had missed the bag completely and that it had fallen onto the seat. I sat back and enjoyed the music.

Over the tannoy I heard "The next stop will be Bicklesford, change here for the Hickton line."

Gathering up my belongings I prepared myself for the stop. It was only by chance that I saw the Dictaphone. I picked it up and returned it to my handbag.

A few days later I decided to play the recording before going to visit Gran.

"... the meeting will be on the 15th. No scrap that typist, the meeting will be on the 16th, Oh no maybe not forget that will you just say that there will be a meeting held yet to be determined. Thank you, typist."

Although it meant nothing to me, I could understand how this might be an amusing, yet frustrating, shared memory to those in the know. Suddenly, much to my horror, I heard "damn the earplugs." Oh no, I must have pressed the record button when I was retrieving them. I didn't know that it would record over what was already there.

The tape continued in a very low almost inaudible tone but I turned the volume up to full, strained my ears and listened carefully, "I told you I did it. I killed Bob. Junior was asked to do it but he chickened out at the last minute saying he couldn't take a life so I had to do it. I wanted to *make it as painless as possible so gave him… The next stop will be Bicklesford, change here for the Hickton line."* I jumped at the unexpected loudness.

I rewound the Dictaphone and played it again. I had heard right. He did say he killed Bob.

I could feel my heart starting to pound. What should I do? Should I tell the police and say I've evidence of a murder? If I do then they are sure to ask me about the two men.

What can I remember about the only two people sitting in the compartment well behind me? If only I had noted them when I rose from my seat. But why should I? It would only have been staring and I didn't realise then that's what I should have done.

I did notice that the one sitting near the window was the larger of the two and that he was wearing a black beanie. I'm not sure whether he had a beard or whether it was stubble or maybe he just had a dark complexion. The slighter man next to him was very pale. I didn't have time to look further because the train was now pulling in to the station. On reflection he did have that pasty look of someone about to faint. I think he had mousy coloured hair although I couldn't be sure because he too was wearing a hat. A woolly one with the brim rolled back. I think it may have had a badge on the front. Yes, I'm certain it did. It was predominantly light blue with some dark blue in the pattern. Or was it the other way around? I can't remember now but I feel confident that it was two shades of blue. The badge that is. The hat was black, I think. It was definitely a dark colour.

I wrote all that I could remember on a notepad in case the police asked me about them.

Perhaps, it's a good thing I didn't take too much notice of them. They might have followed me and… and what?

I shuddered. "Don't be so bloody stupid. It might not have been a murder at all. It might have been their dog, or cat. Lots of people call their pets Bob." I scolded myself. "It may have been some other pet that Junior can't kill. The very name Junior suggests he's only a child."

What I needed most was a stiff drink to stop me shaking but I only had mulled wine in the house and I didn't fancy that. I only drink mulled wine at Christmas parties and this was neither Christmas nor a party. I put the kettle on. I don't usually sweeten my drink but I added two spoons of sugar to my tea because I heard that it was good for shock. It tasted disgusting but I persevered.

By the time I had finished the sickly drink I was rational once more. Surely if they had murdered somebody they wouldn't be discussing it on public transport so it must have been a pet. This thought kept me happy for a while. I placed the Dictaphone and the pad in a drawer.

Nagging doubts started to creep in. What a dilemma. I took a couple of deep breaths in through my nose and breathed out through my mouth. "If a man named Bob had been murdered then I'm sure I would have heard about it by now." I spoke out loud giving myself the same advice I would give to someone else. "Think how daft I would feel if it turned out to be the goldfish," I reassured myself.

I decided not to visit my Gran. I wouldn't be in the right frame of mind. Throughout the day the conversation on that recording kept jumping in and out of my mind.

I spent some time mulling over whether or not I should give the Dictaphone to her at all. However, I knew Gillian would ask Gran if she had listened to Barry Pearce's tape when she wrote her weekly letter and that Gran would answer quite truthfully that she had no idea what she was talking about. That might upset Gillian even more if she thought Gran had forgotten. On the other hand, Gran may have forgotten that she'd received a letter. I felt wicked when I hoped that this was the case. Logic told me that wouldn't happen however, because the care staff always reminded her of the letters she had received.

Also, although I was sure they weren't talking about a murder – but what if? It didn't merit thinking about. I placed the Dictaphone back in the drawer.

I decided to leave it behind when I visited Gran. Mainly because I was nervous of her learning that I had erased part of the dictation and then telling Gillian. Especially as I said I would take care of it. Luckily at that visit it wasn't mentioned at all.

All thoughts of the Dictaphone had faded when Mum visited me a couple of weeks later.

"I've been to see your gran and I was reading the letters that Gillian had sent her. There was a mention of a Dictaphone. Needless to say, your gran knew nothing about it, or couldn't remember where she'd put it. I hunted high and low and care staff also helped me look, well for a short time anyway. They too couldn't remember seeing it and asked what it looked like. I said I don't know I've never seen it before. I said I'd have to ask you. They are now asking the night staff to look out for it…"

I retrieved the Dictaphone and my notes from the drawer as she was talking.

"What on earth is it doing there? Why didn't you take it to her?"

I explained about accidently re-recording over the original and was nervous of what Gillian would say. I played the recording to her.

Upon hearing about the killing of Bob she went a deathly shade of white.

Thinking she was about to faint I sat her down and stupidly asked "Are you all right Mum? Do you want some sugar in your tea?"

She all but collapsed on the chair. "Don't you read the news?"

"Only what comes up on my phone or tablet."

"That's the trouble with the young nowadays. They read the headlines on their phones and think they're up-to-date with everything that's going on. You should watch the six-o-clock news or read a newspaper to get more depth behind the headlines."

"What are you going on about?" I was unhappy with the accusation.

"On the local news about a month ago there was a piece about a young lad named Bob who was murdered by a drugs gang. They are looking for a thick set man with a close dark beard."

It was my turn to turn white.

"It all came to light when 17-year old Junior was rushed to hospital having been badly beaten up and left for dead. He was found by a dog walker. The police said they didn't understand it because he wasn't known to them and there seemed to be no motive."

Mum grabbed my hand. "I remember seeing on the telly one of the men saying he knew nothing about it. He said that he had only met the stocky bloke at the station and was just walking to the train with him. He was a skinny man wearing a navy-blue woolly hat with a two-shaded blue badge of some football club. They were both caught on the station's CCTV."

I took all the information I had to the police who were able to enhance the taped mumblings. It was then used as evidence. It transpired that they tried to kill Junior, a 6ft amateur boxing champion, because he said he was just a delivery boy not a murderer and he didn't want to be more involved than he is. They were frightened Junior would talk. Which, of course, he did.

24

The stocky man received life imprisonment for both murder and drug dealing. The skinny man was jailed for three years for withholding valuable evidence and drug dealing. Junior got nine months in a young offender's institute for drug offences.

When the Dictaphone was with the police I did have to own up and tell Gillian the truth. She thought the whole situation quite amusing and said that she had never realised that one of Barry Pearce's tapes could be so exciting. Upon its return she listened to the re-recorded part again and again before stopping the tape where the confession ended. "There's more than enough for Vivienne to hear that it is Barry. Take it to her to listen to, but I suggest you start at the end of your recording."

This I did. Gran was in fits of laughter all the way through Barry Pearce's dictation although she did say it wasn't funny at the time. In fact, it was very annoying. She told me about all the women she worked with in that office. Sadly, she kept asking if I had to type many of his dictations. It was easier to say that I was lucky enough not to have suffered his ramblings than to explain that I wasn't even born then.

About the author
Linda has had stories published on the Café Lit website plus in the Café Lit anthology. She has also had articles printed in papers and won a prize for journalism although she is not a professional journalist. Her favourite form of writing though is monologues for which she has also won prizes.

Family History

Jim Bates

"So how's little Ronnie?" Sara asked. She loved talking to her daughter, especially since her first baby had arrived earlier in the year. The distance between where Julie lived in California and where Sara and Sean lived in Minnesota didn't seem so great as long as they could connect by phone.

"He's doing really good, Mom. He's over that cold and getting into everything. As usual."

Sara laughed, "Just like you used to do, sweetheart."

Julie smiled inwardly and ignored the comment as she deftly changed the topic, "So, how's Dad doing?"

Sara turned somewhat pensive. "He's good. Okay. You know, staying busy."

"Still in a lot of pain?

"Yeah. That drunk driver not only shattered his hip but drove over him, if you can imagine. It's taking forever to heal. Doctor Adams said it'll probably be painful to some degree for the rest of your dad's life."

"Friggin' drunk."

"No kidding." The line went silent, both mother and daughter thinking.

Sean had been hit six months earlier while bicycling on the Lucy Line trail near their home in Orchard Lake, a small town west of Minneapolis. The bike trail crossed a well traveled street and Sean had been waiting for traffic to clear when the drunk had lost control of his car and plowed into him. Sean was in the hospital for a month recovering. The drunk was sentenced to a year in prison for his third violation. A small price to pay, in Sara's mind, for almost killing the man she loved.

Julie cleared her throat and picked up the conversation, "How's that ancestry work of his coming along?"

While Sean was recovering he started looking into his family's history. He was a retired history teacher and having a project with historical implications was right up his alley.

"Good. He's starting to make progress."

"Finding out about his ancestors? Our ancestors?"

"Yes. On his mother's side. He's immersed in it right now, working at the dining room table."

"I'll bet he's got stuff scattered all over the place."

Sara laughed. "As a matter of fact he does."

Sean had spent nearly thirty years teaching at the local high school. He was a sucker for historical information and maps in particular. It had only been in the past year since he'd retired that the dining room table had been cleared of all his papers. Until now.

"He belongs to one of those ancestry groups," Sara continued. "It's keeping his mind occupied at least."

"How about you, Mom? How are you doing?"

"Oh, I'm okay." Sara hoped she wasn't too quick to respond. The truth of the matter was she had been feeling a little down lately, but really didn't want to talk to her daughter about it. After all, Julie had a baby to care for; and a job; and a husband; and a life. She brought the conversation back to Sean. "Your dad gets into his moods, that's for sure. Sometimes he withdraws and doesn't really say much. I know it bothers him not to be as active as he once was."

"Still using the cane?"

"Yes. We've also got a wheelchair for him so he can move around better."

"Sounds like you're doing all you can."

Sara smiled. "I am, and we are. But don't you go troubling yourself about your father and me. We're fine."

Which was partly true, but Julie didn't need to know that Sean's drifting and turning inward was putting a strain on their marriage. If only she could do something. But, as the saying went, 'It takes two to tango.' If Sean was withdrawing there was nothing she could do about it except ride it out.

Mother and daughter talked a while longer before hanging up, Sara agreeing to call Julie again in a few days. Then she went looking for Sean, wondering if he was working on his family history.

He was. She found him at the dining room table studying his laptop, a large world atlas lay open to his right, his cane leaning against the table to his left. Sara took a moment to take in the sight of her husband of forty-six years. Sean was just under six feet tall, slightly doughy and nearly bald. He was dressed in black jeans and a dark blue and white plaid shirt. His closely trimmed bead was mostly grey and gave him a scholarly look, especially with the wire-framed glasses he'd worn since his late thirties.

She smiled. He was a good man and she loved him dearly, even if he was given to obsessing about things to the point of not sleeping some nights; just like he was with the recent project of his – the family history.

"Hi sweetheart," she said coming up behind him, bending and giving him a hug. "How goes the research."

He turned and hugged her back. "Fantastic." Right away Sara sensed a change had come over him. A change for the good.

"What's going on?" she asked, straightening up and looking at the papers strewn across the table.

He smiled and pointed to some printouts, "Sara, this is amazing. I've been finding out some great information. Guess where my ancestors are from?

Sara pulled up a chair and sat next to him. "I have no

28

clue. You're last name is Nieminen so I always thought from somewhere in Finland."

Sean grinned. "They are, on my dad's side. But on my mom's side they're from Scotland. In fact, they're from an island off the western coast called the Isle of Mull. Apparently I come from a family of crofters. They were like tenant farmers and they raised sheep. I found out about them through some old church records in Tobermory, the biggest town on the island." He sat back and smiled wide, "Pretty cool, huh?"

Sara hadn't seen her husband so excited in months, not since before the accident. His enthusiasm energized her, actually making her flush in happiness.

"How about if I make us some tea and you can tell me more about it?"

"That'd be great," he smiled and reached for her hand and pulled her to him. "I'm super excited." He kissed her passionately and it took her only a moment to come to grips with the old Sean coming back to her. But only a moment. She liked what she saw. And felt.

She kissed him in return and then said, "I'll get the tea and be right back."

"Hurry," he said and turned to his laptop. "This is fun."

Sara went into the kitchen and fixed a tray with two cups of English Breakfast tea and a plate of shortbread cookies. She brought them out to the dining room and set the tray on the table after moving some paper printouts aside.

"So, what'd you find?" She sat next to him.

Sean tapped a few keys and pulled up a chart he'd put together. "Look at this. I traced Mom's family back five generations to Scotland. After that, records are hard to find. Most of them were kept in churches and in many cases they were lost due to fires. I was lucky with Mom's side that the church in Tobermory stayed intact all these years."

"What's the family name?"

"Mom was a MacDonald. Nice and Scottish, isn't it?"

"It is." Sara smiled and sipped her tea. "You know, I've heard about Mull. They've got eagle colonies on that island. White tailed eagles. People visit them from all over the world."

Sean took a sip from his cup and munched on a cookie. "It seems like a cool place. It's the fourth largest of the Scottish Islands. It's got three hundred miles of coastline. It's got a population of just under three thousand." He turned to his laptop. "Here, let me show you this." Sean started up YouTube. "I found a video, kind of a travel-log about the island. It's ten minutes long. You want to watch?"

"Absolutely." Sara was excited that Sean was excited, but she was also looking forward to finding out more about a place that sounded so interesting.

The video showed rolling hills, windswept shorelines, quaint towns and villages, stone crofts and some interesting geologic features. And the eagles, of course. Sara was an avid birdwatcher and they drew her attention. "You know, Sean," she said, after the video was over, "it might be fun to go there. Check out the island, look into your ancestors and see where they lived. I'd love to see the eagles."

Sara was glad he didn't immediately disagree. Instead, he sat back and thought for a minute, munching on another cookie. Then he said, "I don't know. Getting around is hard with this damn hip. I'd have to take my wheelchair and my cane. Going through airport security would be a pain," he laughed. "No pun intended."

Sara grinned. With his mood improving, she could easily talk him into going. "You remember when my friend Ellen and her husband traveled to Europe a few years ago? She took her wheelchair and it worked out fine. Security wasn't a problem. She said the main issue was that it was all in her head. When she finally realized that people traveled all the time with a variety of special needs she was good to go, and they went ahead and did it. The airport staff was really helpful. In fact, she said that everyone they met was kind and generous. By the time she and her husband got to Europe all was going smoothly."

"I just wish I didn't feel like such a cripple."

"Don't start feeling sorry for yourself," she admonished. "You're alive. You've got me, and Julie and little Ronnie. You've got a good life, Sean. You need to remember that. Make the most of it."

Sara enjoyed telling her husband exactly how she felt. She was tired of pussy footing around his feelings. He was an adult. Let him hear the truth.

Sean was quiet, thinking. His ears had turned red, a sure sign he was embarrassed. "I guess I have been kind of a jerk lately."

"Not so much a jerk, just withdrawn and not yourself." She reached over and rubbed his bald head affectionately. "Time to get with the program, babe. There's a lot of living to do."

He was quiet then, thinking, which in Sara's mind was a good thing. He was an introvert by nature and needed to feel comfortable when making a decision, no matter how big or little it might be. In the end, it had to make sense to him.

Finally he laughed.

"What's so funny?" Sara asked, sensing something good was coming.

"Well, I found out that in Scotland a high point of land is called a mull. If we went to the island, like we're talking about, we could search for those eagles and look around and get a feeling about where my ancestors came from."

"Yeah, that's right. It'd be fun. What's so humorous?"

"Well, I'm mulling over going to Mull to walk on a mull. It's kind of funny when you think of it."

Sara laughed. "When you put it that way it is."

"And you know what," Sean said, reaching out to hold his wife's hand, "when you put it that way, we should do it. We really should go."

"You're sure?"

"Yeah. Enough mulling it over. Let's go to Mull."

Sara hugged her husband. "I'm with you, babe. I can't wait." They held each other for a moment and then she added, "You know what? Maybe I should go out and buy something to mark the occasion." She looked at him coyly, "Maybe some mulled wine?"

Sean burst out laughing, "That's a great idea. We're going on an adventure so we should celebrate. In fact," he stood up and reached for his cane, "I'll go with you."

About the author

Jim lives in a small town twenty miles west of Minneapolis, Minnesota. In addition to Cafélit, his stories have appeared in over two hundred online and print publications. His collection of short stories *Resilience* is scheduled to be published in 2020 by Bridge House Publishing. His story *Aliens* was nominated for the 2020 Pushcart Prize in fiction. All of his stories can be found on his blog at:
www.theviewfromlonglake.wordpress.com.

Her Time

Sally Angell

It seemed so clear-cut, the dividing line. You couldn't wait to be on the other side, an endless blue sky window. The possibilities, all the things you could do or be were mulling deliciously round in your mind. Freedom at last!

Yeah. Right.

"There's no record of my details?" In panic, you'd knocked the phone and it was swinging mid-air. You grabbed at the twizzled wire, swearing. Some helpline. "I emailed the forms. Definitely."

"You'll have to apply again."

"No!" You inhaled frantically, trying to hold onto those lovely dreams: the scent of grass on country walks, leisurely mornings in cafés; afternoons reading novels, hourless, minuteless peace…

"Ah." Sounds of tapping keys. "Yes. Ms – Regan? Sor – ry. Computer blip."

"So I'm good to go?" A whoosh of relief.

"Absolutely. We just need your documents now."

"They were attached." Your heart dropped. Any more stress and you'd be dead before the date of your release anyway. The lines of your next life chapter would remain unwritten.

The daily performance went on, one call-centre voice swearing one thing, another the opposite, them losing information, losing the plot. And you trying to edit all their incompetences and mistakes. What a mess.

It was tiring. And in your brain, the question circled. Will it happen, won't it, what you've been longing for so long? With each calendar square ticked off, the red-letter date edged closer. And of course, everyone knew.

"Hello, soon-to-be lady of leisure." Your daughter

sounded tinny on her mobile, when she phoned to ask you to collect Millie from playschool. You couldn't miss the 'I'll have a permanent childminder/someone to listen to me moaning' lift in her voice. Typical Leanne.

Your son texted later. "Ma, there's a flat going, near me. The sprogs are so excited, said we'll see Grandma every day."

So ditto the emotional blackmail. Admittedly Mark was shitting himself (his usual choice language), trying to keep going after 'that woman' left him. And the situation *was* sad. You'd started to awake frightened at night, the grandchildren's pain in your head, their tears in your eyes.

But with both your children, there were undertones of how your change of circs would benefit *them.* You couldn't help wondering. They were your kids. Had you made them like that? And of course, there was the niggle that you should want to cater to their every whim.

And then your sister. "We could have a party!" It made you feel sick, as if you'd eaten one of Jane's sugary, over-iced cakes.

"I don't know. We'll see."

You repeated that ad nauseum because you were stuck in limbo, not able to read the next part of the story, yourself. Your stress levels shot sky-high. The thought of having to backtrack, to have to stagger on as before, was bad enough for a gin and under-the-duvet meltdown.

You kept forcing yourself to punch in the dreaded Contact Us digits every day. You had to. And once a lad whooped that he'd found them, the papers, in a separate software file. Yay! But the next time, a surly girl was adamant. No, madam, nothing.

You picture creeping into the office, and your line manager's smirk.

"Changed your mind, Molly? You *can* stay on, you know."

As if. She'd said that when you notified her originally.

You don't have to leave. Did she really not get it? And your colleagues, particularly the younger ones, had been so concerned for your mental health.

"But what will you do with your time, Molly?" they asked in wonder. "Gardening?" As if you'd rebirth into Molly Titchmarsh, and tell petunias from weeds, magic cat poo from the fungus patch that is your lawn, and become landscaper of the year. Were they mad? But you could hardly reveal your naughty secret, that you were *ecstatic* at the thought of escaping the daily mind-numbing obligations, and escaping from *them*.

Did they really not see that you had a hidden self? Lazy Molly. You were, in fact, a slob who had to practise mirror-work intensely before breakfast, and use a bucket of product to turn your face and body into Molly at Work.

There'd been smug nods from friends, veteran retirees. "You'll get bored out of your brain."

I won't.

"You don't want to watch daytime telly. Oh no. Don't do that."

It was exasperating, everyone telling you what to do, think, feel. But you had dared to believe the fantasy that sustained you through the robotic days and killing early morning starts. And you'd started to imagine living as you were meant to live.

You'd been waiting for this moment of escape, you realized all your life. Perhaps from birth though you didn't know it then. It was the first time, it hit you, that you'd be able to do what *you* wanted. Even in girlhood, you had to play to your role in the family. Molly is like this, like that. Children have to fit into their parents lives. And as adults, we have to please bosses, partners, children.

Well no more. No more living to other people's rules, you'd thought. This time you'd be writing the script, and directing and acting it too. And you were nearly there.

Exhausted, but nearly there. Just had to keep going, you'd told yourself. Just a few more weeks, a few more days...

But now you couldn't get a human being on the call-centre line, just mindless muzak on loop. A chill crept permanently round your body. It was your right to have an efficient rite-of-passage.

You couldn't do it all again, what you'd been doing for years, energy spread too thinly. You couldn't keep it all together any more. Something would give. Something in your body, your mind, your emotions, your soul, would break.

You'd had enough. Like all those other women, women born in your era, you were incensed at changes none of you were warned of, worried about health and money, and quite simply worn out.

Jane has insisted you do lunch. She's smugly telling you your coffee has slopped into the saucer. So you slop it some more and she shudders, dabbing at the puddle on the table with paper serviettes until it's soaked up. She wipes her hands carefully and sniffs, the hair in her nostrils wobbling. You've got nothing in common really. Now the children are grown, it's obvious how different you are, how you irritate each other.

But, hey, you should feel carefree! And you do. The sudden notification had arrived just as you'd given up hope, informing you about the income and other entitlements and freebies you'll get from now on.

"Isn't this nice?" Jane sips her hot chocolate. "We can spend time together now you're retired."

Help! You take your mind back to that last day. You were on a high, floating out of the workplace gates for the last time. And after that it was Bank Holiday, only this time never having to go back to normal life. It was bliss, waking up naturally, never mind all that circadian rhythm nonsense. You could lie in, and it was wonderful. Not having to do anything. Not having to be anywhere. Until today.

"I could come and stay next week." Jane beams. (*You can entertain me now I'm an empty nester*).

"I'm away then."

"Doing what?" Above the scrutinizing gaze, the thick greytone eyebrows skew into question marks.

"Bookbinding."

It just pops into your head. You haven't actually reserved a place on the course yet. But you'd meant to. The advert was in the Google search you did for ideas, inspiration for activities or holidays you might want to try, to fill all this lovely blank space. Just because you could; no worries about succeeding or failing, just pleasure and leisure, you told yourself. Oh, the wonderful indulgence of enjoying yourself on weekdays.

"Hm. Couldn't you do it another time?" Because, and you see it suddenly, that's what you've always done. What other people want.

"Sadly not. Deposit's non-returnable."

Her eyes gleam. "Perhaps I could come too."

Oh hell.

"It's full."

Well, that's it. You'll just have to do *Bookbinding for Beginners* now.

It's the first day. The tutor's talking about signatures. And you think, ah that's something I understand. That's my language. Signing one's name. The subject had grabbed your interest because it sounded sort of literary and classy. You had visions of the hand-made and illustrated manuscripts of the past, historical ways of recording. All about writing and reading.

Except it isn't. And the signature, in this case, is a group of papers which make up a collection of pages, which hopefully will be made into a book. You stare at the array of tools and of different materials, and diagrams that don't make sense. Kevin, that's his name, notices. "You look puzzled—?"

"Molly. I've never been good at practical things."

He starts a group demo, of what to do first – "It's easy," which makes you feel a bit thick. Then there is the mull which looks like a piece of rough cloth, sort of weaved, which will be glued under the book covers.

"Mull." You roll the sound round, you press your tongue to the roof of your mouth so the sound's almost glottal. M u lllll. "Isn't it funny?" Chatter, chatter, as if you are not a grown-up (well a post-grown-up), but about six, in school again. "How words can sound the same but have different meanings? Mulling it over. Mull is to fail or make a mess of. The island of Mull. I like words. I like writing."

"Ri – i – g – ht." Kevin dodges the thingy you're waving around. "Don't cut yourself, Molly, with that Exacto knife!"

The what? And which way up did you hold the damn thing?

But by the post-lunch session (a lunch accompanied by potent mulled wine being trialled early), the ideas, the instructions, the processes of this craft have fermented in your brain, and started to make sense. The workroom settles into a sepulchral peace. Through your daydreams the muted sounds of breathing, and a woody smell, are relaxing. Winter sun from the window pools on the tabletop, and dazzles round your head. You lose yourself in the making; making something new, that you are creating, something of your own.

As you stick and stitch, you think how our lives are like a piece of fabric, plain and perfect but then shaped by other hands which cut it and pull it, and stitch it into their own patterns.

Muffled pings from your phone are like soft clouds in a calm sky. The real world outside of this room doesn't exist. Nor the people in it. If your phone screen lights up, letters or numbers appear like a foreign lingo.

The next morning, the programme says Evaluation.

"This is your book," Kevin says reverently. "You can design it how you like. Some of you brought family history printouts, but if you've done blank pages that's OK too. You can do journalling, handwrite stories or poems, or draw illustrations in it."

The books are displayed, and you like how yours looks. Who said you couldn't make things? Where did the idea come from? Who planted that belief in your being? Hell, of course you can do practical stuff. You've done it for years at work, in life. And you remind yourself, of the affirmation you learnt at the self-care group you went to last week, to see if you liked it.

"The past is gone. You are a blank canvas."

You're fired up, travelling home on the train. And you like this, this idea of travelling, being on the road, going places. Not having to get back for work. There are messages on your phone, but you don't want to break the spell of your own private retreat. There is one number that dings in your brain, but you can't place it.

Home. A bubble bath, and into your jim-jams, and then the messages ping in. How did it go? Did you meet anyone? Can I see what you made? You haven't had a lot of contact with relatives in recent years. You went to your job in the daytime, slept and went shopping weekends. The occasional visit. But now they're thinking, 'Oh! She's available.' And you start to worry. Have you swapped one set of expectations for another?

You wake that night in a dread sweat. Sit up straight as a ruler, hearing your mother's voice, the brain-stained dialogue repeating. You are back there, in childhood. "You must think of *Other People*. You must help *others*." You got the message. Everyone else is more important.

When she died, the emotional blackmail still had the power to get to you. You remember the eulogies.

"Alice always put others before herself."

But that was how mum was, what *she* was like. Or, since the whole generation of women in that age group seemed to be of the same mould, it was how they were, in *their time*.

"Boundaries." Julia announces today's theme. It's the next Tuesday, at the Self-Care and Wellbeing Group. You've checked the programme, not sure about committing to going each week. You'll have to get up more quickly and be compos mentis to be with other people. But this topic, well, it was meant for you. It's a sign.

"We are not our mothers," Julia emphasizes. "We have to stop being people-pleasers, stop worrying what people think of us, and make our own choices. Do what makes *us* happy."

Then everyone's talking over each other. But my family won't do boundaries! Trouble is, they're nice people. But they think they own my life. I can't say No to them because there'll be this great big *drama*, and they'll say I'm a nasty person.

"Well, it will be dramatic." Julia's head nods vigorously. "You are trying to break free of the brainwashing we all go through from our parents and teachers and society."

You feel buoyant as you go home. It's not just you, then. Come on, Molly. You can do this. You can set border lines. Oh, the time spent thinking out the right words, the most effective tone. How to breathe. Because they can get to you, those close to you, push your buttons.

You practice in the mirror as Julia said.

"Strike a superwoman pose. And say it. Out loud."

You throw your head and arms back, and stick your chest out.

"NO!" No. No No.

Your daughter turns up on the doorstep the next morning. And the next. This wasn't what it was supposed to be, your life after life, you fret, when she leaves Millie with you while she disappears to the shops. This part of the story, your third act, was meant to be written only by you.

Millie is playing in that way children do, in the moment, being and doing just as she feels. You watch her giving a little twirl, standing thumb in mouth, daydreaming, and your heart catches. She falls asleep in your lap, and you breathe in her baby smell. You put your hand on her flushed cheek. You want to see her, and them. But not all the time. You must have your own space.

Leanne comes back, and you say it.

"I haven't got time for this."

Leanne looks puzzled. "But you've got all the time in the world now."

"No. I've done all this for years, when you were little. I have to live my life now, living as *I* want to." Oh hell. You can see what she's thinking from the familiar pout. *How Selfish.*

Later, you have Jane on the phone, wanting you to meet up with people from half a century ago, because she lives on planet nineteen-fifties. You repeat your mantra, and you hear the thickness of tears when you tell her no. You open a bottle of wine, take a swig. This is doing your head in. Your back is hurting. But you cannot let guilt get to you.

Mark emails about his ex working extra hours for two weeks so she can't have the children, and can you go and stay to mind them? "Because I have a bloody job too."

You feel as if you've been turned inside out. And it's too much. You nearly say you will pay for a childminder for that time, but he's rung off.

41

You've done it! The sensation is strange. Stopping the yes, yes, yessing. Putting yourself first. But you're not going to slip back.

You don't recognize the figure on the doorstep. At first.

"Hello Molly."

Oh hell. The mysterious phone call while you were away. You put his face to the number. Peter. You go to slam the door but he stands in the way.

"I'm sorry I haven't been in touch. I've had shingles."

Well, his face does look like a shiny red-skinned tomato.

"Can I come in?"

"Why did you ghost me?"

He didn't, he said. He lost his phone with your number in, and then started itching. So that was how important you were, that he hadn't safe-guarded your details.

"But you called." That day on the course.

"I found it." He looks at his shoes. "In the garage."

You shrug.

"I just need to sit down. Car's packed up. I got the bus."

You sigh. It's difficult, this dating. The men all have historical ideas of what women should be and are for. And really you realize, you just like going out to lunch, and perhaps a hand to hold walking round. It's comforting, nice to have a bit of attention, do things together sometimes.

"I just want to be friends with someone first."

"Can I have a glass of water?"

You fetch it. He pats your arm.

"Shall we go upstairs then?"

You glare.

"I was joking!"

You lean against the wall when he's gone. You're getting used to being in control, to thinking of yourself. To being who you really are.

42

Who is she then, this real self? You're reminded of those Russian dolls, one inside the other, all different, all part of each other. You think of all the women you have been, or could have been, All the Mollys – Molly the daughter, student, the mother, wife. You remember having imposter-syndrome when someone called you Mrs, as if you didn't recognize yourself. All the labels you'd been given. Molly, the divorcee, lover, partner, widow, business woman, employee, grandma.

So who are you? Who is the real you? She's the inner you, the person you are deep inside. You. Yourself. The one you were in the beginning. And you will find her.

You're not telling the old story any more. Or believing other people's viewpoints, how they see you. Everything you do is by choice, and you are always free to choose again.

You're almost scared to look for the book you made, recalling the thick cream pages, blank, to be filled by you. Molly, Part three. Your third age.

This is not for someone else. It's for you. Your words. There are no wrong ones, just how they fall. Each mark, each moment, each breath, just as it is. Your pen meets the paper, the ink flowing as if from your hand as you write:

My Time

About the author
Sally Angell loves literature and writing, and is always aiming to develop new and original ideas in her writing. Sally explores the truth and reality of feelings, the originality of language and the possibilities of words. She likes to write stories with contemporary themes, that also have a universal meaning. Her writing has been published in anthologies and magazines, and read on radio. A story first published back in 1989 is to be republished for Christmas 2020 by K T Publications in a book of ghost stories.

Into the Shade

L. F. Roth

Bent over his toast, Bill doesn't bother to look up as she joins him in the kitchen. I've reached the B-side of my life, she thinks. Next month, she will be sixty-two to Bill's sixty-five. The cover of an EP appears, fittingly, before her eyes, and she turns it over. Track three: "Growing Apart." Actually, the flipside of a single would be more appropriate, given the state of their relationship: last week, making their beds, she had found a sticky hankie under his. In the early days, it would have been a used condom – an unnecessary precaution, they learned, when he finally agreed to start a family. The A-side had held disappointments, too.

"How's it going?" she asks, referring to his recent acquisition.

He grunts.

And that is it.

Mind you, in a way she has herself to blame. She should have been happy he had hit upon something to occupy him. But his choice had taken her by surprise. In their thirty years together, he has never planted even an orange pip.

She had echoed him, cutting short his explanation: "An allotment."

"I always wanted a garden."

His expression implied this couldn't be news to her.

"To grow what?"

He had been vague, confirming her scepticism. She doubted he could tell a turnip from a swede.

The allotment had come late, not merely in his life but in the season too. Due to some misunderstanding between the previous holder and the council, he didn't get to sign the contract until a week ago, when summer was half over. He has tried to make up for it, picking up the necessary tools in something of a rush, googling for seeds that might still produce a crop. In the sitting room, on sheets of newspaper, are potatoes, placed there for eyes to form. He must have begun digging, creating beds, but she hasn't been down to look. "Give me a week or two," had been his suggestion.

Today, Nola decides not to. He has had three full days – she should show an interest. After packing a picnic lunch, she sets off. She knows where the allotments are and expects to find his without problems.

But he is nowhere in sight. "Bill Lowell?" she enquires of a man crouching by a bed of beans alternating with beets – it is midweek and there aren't many people around. "I wonder if you…?"

A headshake. She moves on, striking first one path, then another. The area is larger than she had imagined, having glimpsed it only from the bus, and here and there bushes and tall plants form hedges that obstruct the view. Mostly, she notes, the separate plots, some the size of their flat, others twice that, are well cared for, exhibiting a profusion of flowers and vegetables. This must be what Bill has envisaged. One or two have not been worked. There the grass grows knee-high and thistles, cow parsley and nettles flourish. Around the borders, marked by low posts she can barely make out, dandelions have gone to seed. In one, a corner has been dug over; a spade, brand new by the looks of it, is stuck in the ground, abandoned. The clods have not been broken up. Roots of grass and weeds bind them together. Could this be Bill's? If that is the case, he has got his work cut out for him.

On the ground there is a pair of gardening gloves, equally anonymous.

She sees him throwing them down in disgust, his enthusiasm dulled with the monotony of the task.

What should she do? Near the entrance to the area, she

had spotted a bench and a quick walk takes her there. She will have her picnic lunch regardless. Spreading a paper napkin beside her, she sets out what she had meant for them to share and for an instant she is back at the hospital canteen where she had worked. Sandwiches and tea was all he ever ordered. Then, as he disposed of his lunch, she used to observe him furtively from behind the counter, fascinated by his hands, strong but nimble, fit for a bigger man. They had reminded her of her grandfather, who'd always made her feel safe. Bill's outfit showed that he was an orderly. In addition, apparently, he helped to set broken bones, preparing the plaster. It was close to a year before he asked her out.

"I'm getting a divorce," he had told her, placing her drink in front of her.

Not an auspicious beginning: Nola hadn't been aware he had a wife. Raising her glass, she had taken a sip but offered no comment. He had expected none.

"I'm leaving you," the wife had announced, out of the blue. "I'm pregnant, but that's not why. I would have left you anyway. The child is Jeff's."

Was that his name? Jeff? Nola couldn't swear to it. No matter. Whatever it was, he had been Bill's best man at the wedding.

Bill had gone over the scene, his eyes distant. The one he missed most, evidently, was Jeff.

And she had listened, studying his hands; the right one spun his glass around, spilling not a drop.

Now Nola pours tea from the flask. It is a little weak, which is how Bill prefers it.

"This was some time ago?" she had proffered.

It was not: his wife's side of the bed had not even gone cold the day he approached Nola – though that was not how he had phrased it.

46

A substitute, she had concluded, given a walk-on part until someone else auditioned for the role; wary, she had been ready to drop him on the spot.

But they had gone on meeting and not exclusively at work. For months she put off introducing him to her family. "You seeing anyone?" her mother had quizzed her, casually, and she had denied it: "No one special." Which involved no lie.

It needn't have developed beyond that – in actual fact, the night he proposed, there had been nothing to signal what was coming.

Nola finishes her sandwich and packs up her things. She could have refused him. Supposing she had, where would she have been today? Would she have had children? Grandchildren? She conjures up an image of herself entering a park, one or two toddlers in tow, instead of helping someone steer a walker down a corridor, trying to keep up a conversation. She doesn't imagine herself on the cover of Vogue or, for that matter, married to a hospital director. Her prospects had been limited. Fingering her fourteen-carat ring, she wonders how Bill's ex-wife has made out. Has she too arrived at the B-side of her life?

On her return, Bill meets her in the door.

"Where have you been?"

His eyes go to the bag in her hand.

"I could ask you the same."

She heads for the kitchen. He follows her but stops in the doorway to watch her unpack flask, mugs, leftover sandwiches.

"Picnicking," he concludes.

"You can have yours here."

"You went over to the allotment?"

She nods. He sits down at the table and removes the

47

wrapping from the sandwiches. Having picked one up, absentmindedly, he puts it down to pour some tea.

"I've been to Woolford's."

She must have revealed her ignorance.

"The garden centre," he explains. "You can hire a tiller for under fifty pounds. That's for one day. But one day should do it."

"A tiller," she repeats.

"To turn over the soil."

The spade and the gloves.

"Is it that hard?"

"No one's worked it for a year." He scowls. "Beats plaster of Paris. The tiller would break it up."

He isn't requesting permission, is he? The allotment is his.

"Sounds like a good idea."

But he was merely informing her: he had arranged for its delivery while in town.

And had it been a good idea? Yes and no. The tiller loosened the soil, it was true, but – this he let slip – it killed few of the weeds. In part, that was because he didn't dispose of the seeds that had formed prior to his going over the ground, in part because simply chopping up the roots wasn't sufficient – some began to grow anew. Couch grass, which to her sounded innocent enough, seemingly did. Others, like dandelions, grew from well below the reach of the tiller. He takes it in his stride.

For some weeks she sees little of him. Late in the afternoon, his self-assigned chores completed, he settles down to catch the news on TV once supper is over. Mostly he dozes off within minutes.

He traces his progress on the plan he has drawn. "I sowed beans here." He points to the word. "And beets.

They're good for each other. The beans provide nitrogen for the beets."

He has memorized the instructions on the seed packets and reels them off: "Carrots. A foot between rows. Seeds an inch apart. Cover with a quarter inch of fine soil. Thin them in stages." If she were to wake him through the night and whisper: "Lettuce. Radishes. Onions. Chives. Marrows. Swiss chard," he would feed her the information for each. He finishes one bed at a time, hacking at the soil with spade and trowel, marking out drills – "Drills?" she mumbles – sowing and watering before he moves on to the next. The potatoes go in last, row upon row, in early August, months beyond the optimal date. By then, radishes and beans are beginning to sprout, he tells her. And weeds. Trowel in hand, he clears both beds and paths once more.

Nola follows her own routine: a companion to old people on Tuesdays and Thursdays, she also volunteers in a kitchen every second week.

"Want to get a bit of sunshine?" She smiles at Mrs. Parnell. "It's a lovely day."

Mrs. Parnell, formerly a staff nurse, is one of Nola's three regulars, whom she has collected for walks, weather permitting, since she herself retired at sixty. Will this be her in twenty years, plodding along behind a four-wheeled walking frame, attended by someone in marginally better shape? Will Bill be there for her? Or will she be the one walking him?

Mrs. Parnell remembers her back garden, where her husband raised vegetables. "My flowers had to go in the front, where there wasn't much sun," she has informed Nola. "Still, you can't win 'em all." Today she wants to know how their allotment is coming on. "You must be harvesting any number of things," she declares. "September's around the corner."

And Nola reminds her that Bill had got going late. She herself has called by only once – he gave her the impression that he didn't really want her there. He had progressed so far as to draw up soil around the potatoes – earthed them, was the term he used – but they were not in flower. In fact, nothing else was flowering either, though the beans and the marrows should be, shouldn't they? They seemed reasonably healthy, but small. The sole crop he has brought home consists of radishes, poor crooked things resembling fingers suffering from arthritis. Pitiful, she had thought.

Mrs. Parnell tut-tuts. "Bryn couldn't be bothered with radishes. He wasn't one for salads. He liked things you could cook."

Nola is not about to argue with Mrs. Parnell over her late husband's preferences – or over what fights to take. "Each to his own," she avows and they walk on towards the park where they will find a seat and contemplate the silence. With summer over, there is little birdsong. After a rest, she will escort Mrs. Parnell back to the nursing home.

September draws to a close and Bill brings Nola a handful of French beans – housework is her responsibility. She inspects them with suspicion: covered in black specks, they are nothing like the ones that graced the seed packet. Has some parasite been at work?

Bill shrugs. "You're not going to serve them raw, are you?"

He claims that cooking them will kill whatever has been there – his past work taught him to trust the sterilizer. And to Nola's surprise, the specks disappear the moment the beans are plunged into boiling water. Come suppertime, she nibbles at one, with no noticeable ill effects.

Was that the time she had asked if he had ever heard from Jeff? It could have been.

"Jeff?" he had replied. "No. Why?"

But not overly curious, she had abandoned the subject.

He delivers more beans, equally speckled, but little else. The onions he had tried to grow from seeds have come to nothing – you had to start them off in January, he was told, or else plant sets, and that, too, early in the year. The beets are minuscule and twisted; in that respect not unlike the radishes, with dents and hollows that make it well-nigh impossible to slip off the skin. The chard wilts as it grows. Now, with less weeding and watering to do, Bill spends much of his days on the Internet and divulges that one reason his marrows won't flower might be that he didn't give them sufficient room to grow. He thins them out and in the end one plant produces fruit – but this is in October and a light frost kills what flowers remain.

Nola, invited down, examines the devastation.

"The potatoes will make up for it," she assures him.

"What have potatoes got to do with marrows," he mutters.

"Nothing," she could have said; or "Everything."

Unaffected by the cold, they could have been grown for their flowers alone. With five petals that shift from pale violet to white and a remarkably thick orange stalk in the centre – its stamen? – they are a lot prettier than the marigolds that sprout, like an afterthought, at the end of a bed, at most four inches high, fit company for the carrots that share their space – carrots whose ragged tops insinuate that something is sadly amiss down below. Strange bedfellows, she thinks, carrots and marigolds – but then, why not?

"Look good enough to eat," she remarks, indicating the potatoes.

Of course, the opulence of the flowers may not be mirrored underground.

November has arrived. Bill has left the carrots where they are, having learned that they are frost-resistant – hoping for what? – and brings home nothing but lettuce leaves. She rinses them off and puts them in a bowl with sliced tomatoes, but he rarely touches her quick-fix salad. She disposes of her share, with Mrs. Parnell's husband on her mind.

Her days pass routinely. Although the weather is far from inviting, she walks her pensioners each week, convinced fresh air and exercise will do them good; nor does she shirk her kitchen duty. Bill, on those mornings, stays in bed, face to the wall. By the time she returns, he is mostly out somewhere. Her work calls for no special skills. She gives a hand wherever it is required, cleaning pots and pans, doing the dishes, preparing the ingredients for the cook.

"Lil's not in today," Ellen may notify her. "Can you do the potatoes?"

And she ties on her apron and plugs in the potato peeling machine. On such occasions, the allotment will present itself to her view, the delicately coloured petals waving in the breeze.

But it is not at work alone that the allotment makes its presence known. Twice, in a dream, she finds herself bent over the sink, pots and bowls fighting for space. Diminutive, under attack, the potatoes slip out of her hands and roll across the floor. Grabbing one that is slightly larger, she sees it has been tunnelled into. There are holes everywhere. She cuts it in two before dividing it again and again, till nothing remains. In tears, she frees herself from her apron and flings it over a chair. She hears Bill's voice.

"You're leaving."

Her answer is immediate.

"I am."

"The potatoes."

"No. I would have left you anyway."

"For Jeff." He makes a face and turns on his heel.

A man holds out an orange flower. Jeff. That is not what she wants. She backs away.

"Take it," he insists.

But she won't.

In the rerun, there is a small child clinging to the man, but the second she reaches out to welcome it, he fades, and with him the child.

Take it.

The dreams should have been Bill's, not hers.

It is still November when, having walked Mrs. Andrews and Miss Turner, Nola discovers, back in her kitchen, not heaps of potatoes but carrots, whose colour could compete with that of the centre of the potato flowers. Their green tops have been removed. Firm, sturdy, without the slightest blemish, they cover much of the draining board. No trace of soil is left. Bill must have scrubbed them down at the allotment.

Amazed at their perfection, and moved, she searches for a bag under the sink to put them in. Fumbling for one that will be large enough, she catches sight of a receipt in the rubbish bin. Sainsbury's. She stares at it, noting the date, the sum, the purchase. After a deep breath, she pulls herself up straight, but even so feels dizzy and has to lean against the cupboard to regain her balance. Shortly, the carrots are back in focus. Carrots. Put there to tell her what? Confused, she wonders if Bill is out to prove to her his competence: what stands before you is an accredited gardener. Why else get rid of the bag that must have held both carrots and receipt? Or is it the opposite, an admission of failure, bringing a substitute for what he was unable to produce himself? She pulls out a chair and sits herself down. On Bill's side of the cloth there is a mark. She rubs at it with her thumb.

If he claims they are from the allotment, she'll never speak to him again.

With that idea foremost in her mind, she hears his key in the front door. He greets her less casually, with greater reserve, perhaps, than is his custom, and she responds in kind. Upon entering the kitchen, he glances at the draining board. In his hand is a bag from Boots. Shaving gear? Deodorant? He drops it inside the door.

When he speaks, it is to say they have to talk.

"The carrots," she gathers.

But the carrots are incidental.

"They came to nothing," he explains. "The potatoes were puny and full of holes. I just don't have green fingers. Well, you told me that from the first."

"I never did."

"Maybe not in so many words. It doesn't matter. I've given up the allotment. I've terminated the lease. Those carrots" – he nods towards the sink – "I picked them up in town, to mark the end of my delusion. I'm leaving."

He pauses, but the words hang in the air. He is leaving. He has reversed the roles they'd had in her dream.

"Things haven't been right between us for a long time."

"And that's my fault?"

"Yours. Mine. Either way, it's a fact."

She grants him that but is shaken: a woman might leave her husband, but men in their mid-sixties don't walk out on their wives. Thoughts flicker through her mind. Outside a car is starting up, in readiness, it seems, urging him to speed up. She peers at the bag on the floor and in a flash has the scenario worked out. Someone is waiting for him. He has met somebody new, probably down by the allotment. No, not there. In town. Anywhere.

"Who is it?"

Silence fills the room, proving her correct in her conjecture. Most likely the woman will be half his age.

Yet his reply, after a slight delay, startles her.

54

"It's Jeff."

The man he had denied not long ago.

"I came across him on the Internet. Well, I did a search. We've met off and on." He stops, but adds, as if it hardly needs to be spelled out: "The long and the short of it is that I'm moving in with him. It's what I should have done at the outset."

This isn't happening. It makes no sense. She pictures him close the door and sees the flat empty except for some dry, shrivelled carrots by the sink. Beside them are his keys.

"You're leaving," she says.

And other than practicalities, that is it.

"I never even saw a photograph of him," she reveals. "If there was one, he must have had it tucked away somewhere."

Nola is back with her regulars. The birds are tuning up for spring.

"Curiosity killed the cat." Mrs. Parnell sounds triumphant.

It isn't funny, yet the sheer irrelevance of her comment could have sent Nola into fits. It requires an effort for her to control herself.

This is how she has been of late: the smallest thing can set her off, the line thin, a mere gulp, between laughter and tears. Initially, although she knew perfectly well that Bill had walked out on her, she couldn't quite believe it. It was a joke. He was testing her. He would emerge, unexpectedly, out of nowhere, flowers in hand, full of smiles. Then she got angry and her anger lasted for weeks. Who did he think he was? If he were to show up, she would under no circumstances let him in. You made your bed, she would snort. However much he pleaded, she would stay firm. Little by little, though, she mellowed. It may not have been entirely his fault. She could have given him a hand with the allotment; she could have talked to people, found out where he went wrong. Needless to say, it no longer made any difference. That, it seemed, went for most things, with the result that everything she did, she did mechanically. What was the point? She neglected her work. She neglected the flat. She neglected herself. But eventually she rallied; she took in her surroundings and was appalled. He wasn't worth it. No one is.

"Of Jeff, I mean. I never saw his picture, nor met him in person."

"And would you want to?"

She ponders the question. "Perhaps not. But as it is, it's almost unreal. Thirty years of my life blanked out in the blink of an eye."

"There are things best left behind."

"I suppose so."

War, she allows. Famine. Not that she has experienced either. But marriage?

They have reached the park and choose one of the benches in the sun. In a month or two, they will opt for one in the shade. That's age for you.

"This time of year," Mrs. Parnell asserts, "I could sit here all day." She tilts her head. "Hear the birds?"

Nola listens. She nods.

Not all day, she reflects. Not yet. But it will have to do. For the present.

About the author
L. F. Roth has had stories published in competition anthologies brought out by Biscuit Publishing, Earlyworks Press, Bridge House Publishing, Cinnamon Press, AudioArcadia.com, Momaya Press, University of Huddersfield Press, The Plymouth Writers Group, Black Pear Press and Hammond House. They mostly focus on relationships, gender issues and trauma – at times all three. For details and a few excerpts, see https://sites.google.com/site/lfroth1/.

It is Time

Allison Symes

Camilla, by the oval window, watched her daughter barge through the crowds in the mall. Goodness knew where she went wrong with Melissa.

Camilla winced as Melissa scattered several shoppers and their bags. The girl's shouts of "sorry", "didn't see you" and the like didn't endear the human whirlwind to her victims. It didn't impress Camilla she could hear every word. She was on the fifth floor of her apartment block. Melissa's voice *carried*.

Camilla turned away. She may as well make the most of the last moments of calm before Melissa came in. Hopefully the door would stay on the hinges this time.

What should I do? Camilla picked up a glass of prosecco she'd left on the mahogany coffee table and finished it before walking into the hallway, shutting the lounge door behind her.

Melissa was banned from the lounge. It was the only room Camilla had left with anything vaguely nice in it. It was going to stay that way no matter how long or loudly Melissa protested. Yes, it was unfair, but Camilla didn't care. Now was the time to have it out with her daughter. The clumsiness was beyond embarrassing.

Camilla wasn't surprised the reverberations of the front door being shut by Melissa took several minutes to fade. No doubt the neighbours would be along yet again later to complain. No doubt they would also continue their jibes about Melissa's lack of academic achievement.

It would've been nice if I could've said Melissa's clumsiness was a side product of her being a genius. People understand that but no… she is just clumsy and dim.

"Hello, Mother, fancy a coffee?"

"Yes but I'll make it. I don't want you breaking yet another kettle. I got through five last week."

"I said I'm sorry and I did pay for the replacements."

"Yes, dear, out of your redundancy money. I wasn't surprised your firm let you go. I'm only surprised it didn't happen sooner." Camilla turned her back on her daughter and walked elegantly into her kitchen, as if demonstrating how walking should be done.

"Mother, that's unfair. I wasn't the only one to be laid off. There are redundancies happening everywhere. Gary got laid off too and you know how clever he is."

Camilla snorted. Her daughter managed to find a boyfriend who seemed tolerant of her clumsiness, but Camilla thought he was ugly with all the personality of a rock. For one thing, he'd barely spoken five words to Camilla, and then three were swear words.

Why Melissa hadn't thought to warn the idiot her mother was bound not to like that was beyond Camilla, but it was typical. Melissa was so like her late unlamented father.

"So what will you do? There is post. Most look like rejections."

"Thanks, Mother. Some optimism would be nice."

"Prove me wrong then."

Over the coffee, she watched her daughter open the dozen letters, each one being tossed into a bin.

"Don't say it, Mother. I know you're thinking *I told you so* but I've got more applications out there. Something will come up."

"The neighbours are talking…"

"Since when do you listen to them rather than me? I'm clumsy but that's all. There are worse faults. You said you were clumsy as a kid."

"*I* grew out of it. You're twenty-eight. What will you do with your life? You can't keep on like this."

"You want me to move out?"

"No. I think it is time for the clinic."

Camilla wasn't sorry Melissa was sitting. It limited the damage.

"How the bloody hell could you think that? I *am* your daughter, your own flesh and blood. Going to the clinic only happens to failures. I am not one, despite what the bloody neighbours think. Why the hell must I measure up to *their* standards? It's shallow."

Camilla sighed. She wished she'd had a second prosecco now. This was going to be more difficult than she thought.

"By every standard on our world, Melissa, you're a failure and you know it. The clinic, with the appropriate treatment, is your last resort. Everyone has been wondering why I haven't taken you there sooner. It has been *me* pointing out for years people grow out of clumsiness to anyone who cared to listen. Not that they believed me. Now I see why. You haven't done one single thing to improve. Had you been seen to *try,* that would've been something. I can't keep supporting you. The government inspectorate will be round soon. I've had the letter."

Camilla thrust a posh envelope at her daughter. "Go on, read it. If I don't do something about you, *they* will. It would be better for you if they didn't act."

Camilla watched her daughter read the official letter. There had been over 100 complaints about Melissa's accidents in the last month and the inspectorate had given Camilla three options.

Hand her daughter over to them and they would take care of the problem.

Or Camilla could take her to the officially sanctioned clinic.

Or she could hand her over to the Wild Area Zone where the girl could take her chances with whatever it was that lived out there. All that was known about the Wild Area Zone was nobody came out of it alive and those living closest to it reported there were two sounds associated with it – screaming followed by silence.

"See, Melissa, I've got to do something about you."

Melissa put the letter down. "I'll ring Gary, tell him, and then you can take me to the clinic. We'll get this over with. Then you won't have to worry about me anymore. I hope you'll be happy, Mother darling."

Camilla winced. "It's not my fault the government is the way it is. I never voted for them but their *Purity Policy* has been popular."

Melissa swore. "Yes by those who are seen to conform to what is called normal here. You *do* know they feed people to the wolves? *I've* heard the rumours about the Wild Area Zone too. Give me ten minutes."

"I've prepared the official letter for the clinic, Mother, so no more worries! I've given my consent."

"You've sealed the letter. Why didn't you let me check it first? It's important to get this *right*." Camilla reached for her fake fur coat. Her neighbours all had real fur. Melissa had made it clear many times what she thought about that. Camilla liked a quiet life – or as quiet as it could get when your daughter was a clumsy oaf.

"I know it's important, Mother. Of all people, I know! Stop worrying. Now the decision is made, I want to get this right – and I have. Come on, let's go. If I'm going to do this, I want to do it quickly before the nerves set in."

Camilla nodded. That *was* sensible. It was a pity her daughter hadn't been as sensible as that in other areas of her life. Her father hadn't been either. He was one of the first to go to the clinic when the government introduced them.

Every region had at least two clinics, which were always busy. It was funny how undesirables never completely died out on their own accord so the government sped up that process. Their species was to be the best it could be. There was to be no weakness. Clumsiness, of all the things to be sent to the clinic for, was stupid. Melissa deserved this.

Camilla knew she'd have to keep telling herself that until the day she died. Maybe that could drown out the voice in her head telling her not to do this. There was an alternative. Live in the poorer areas. Live like peasants. Be together as a family. Nothing and nobody judging you. Food and resources shared.

It was the live like peasants bit which stopped Camilla. Someone with a name like hers would never get on in such an environment. It was illegal to change your name in this world. The fact it was tattooed on everyone's head shortly after birth made changing it impossible. No tattooist would risk their lives doing so.

For the first time, Camilla wondered about her life choices. But it was too late now. She would have to see this through. The neighbours would stop condemning her. She might even get a reward from the government for 'doing the right thing'.

Melissa walked out of the clinic ten minutes to the second after she entered it. She walked over to a grey car. A young man (who Camilla always thought looked more like an ape than the superior species of human they were supposed to be) got out and kissed Melissa.

"Is it done? Is the cow dead?"

Melissa looked to the chimney above the clinic. There

was smoke coming from it. "Not yet. They won't have had time yet to take her organs and use them for those deemed worthy. There will be some lucky people getting those. Mother had been in excellent health."

"She did this to your father, yes?"

Melissa looked at Gary, tears in her eyes. "He was a nice man. He would've liked you. You'd have liked him. He didn't deserve her. I swore if I got the chance to turn the tables on her, I'd take it."

"What was in your letter?"

"I said Mother was keen on sacrifice for the greater good but rarely put herself forward for anything. Okay, I lied there. You just do what you have to, right? I told them she'd protest but they were to ignore it… What I didn't say was she wanted others to make the sacrifice! All she wanted was her luxury and to fit in with her vicious neighbours. We had many opportunities to live with the poorer folk, who would've made us welcome. If she'd loved Father or me, she would've done that. Draw your own conclusions! I've done this for Father."

"You are more than enough to me, darling."

Melissa gave Gary a jaundiced look. "You *do* know I inherit everything from Mother? She was wealthy."

"Darling, how could you say that? I've been with you through thick and thin and all the verbal abuse that cow threw at you over years."

Melissa nodded. "I'm aware, Gary, there is something I *have* inherited from her. I can be cold when I need to be. I just have been! I've planned this for *years*. Malice aforethought is an understatement here! I reached the point where her barbed comments didn't get to me anymore at least a decade ago. Do you want to be with someone who, if she felt threatened, knows she could do to you what my mother did do to my father and what she attempted to do to me?"

Gary shrugged. "I love you. Now how soon can we get her flat on the market and move out to… Well, where do you want to go? There's a decent commune the other side of Xantris. They're always looking for people who can work with their hands, farming the old way and that kind of thing. We could do that. You could use some of your resources to support us while we get up and running with that and help with their charity work too."

Melissa smiled. "Are you thinking of the *Red Daisy Project*?"

Gary returned the smile. "I can't think of anything better than funding something which will destroy these clinics. Let's have a drink and toast your mother for making it possible."

The pair laughed and walked off into the sunset.

About the author

Allison Symes loves reading and writing quirky fiction. Her two flash fiction collections, *From Light to Dark and Back Again* and *Tripping The Flash Fantastic* are published by Chapeltown Books. She has also been published by Cafelit and Bridge House Publishing. She is a member of the Society of Authors, Chartered Institute of Editing and Proofreading, and Association of Christian Writers.

Her website is at https://allisonsymescollectedworks.com/

She blogs for Chandler's Ford Today often on topics of interest to writers:
http://chandlersfordtoday.co.uk/author/allison-symes/

Her Amazon Author Central page is at
http://author.to/AllisonSymesAuthorCent

and her Youtube channel can be found at
www.youtube.com/channel/UCPCiePD4p_vWp4bz2d8oSJA

Lines of Gold

Margaret Bulleyment

Sylvie stepped off the tram into the fiery avenue of trees that stretched down to Waldemarsudde. Nothing much had changed – not so much autumn, more a fall.

"O to be in Sweden, now that fall is here," she chanted, trudging along in mock-Browning rhythm. Her younger self had obviously never registered the distance to the Royal Park, but it was worth her every ancient step to find the gazebo still there. They must have renewed it over the years she thought, but it looked exactly the same – even without the squirrels. She sat down gently and waited for one to appear.

"Kan jag sitta här?" A young woman with long black shiny hair, stood in front of her.

"Of course you can sit here. Forlåt. Sorry. I understood what you said, but it's been so long since I spoke Swedish I can't even remember the words, let alone put them in sentences."

The woman sat down and opened her lunch box. "That's fine. I love speaking English. My parents made sure we began learning it when we were little. Arabic's my first language."

"Arabic, Swedish and English. That's very impressive. What can I say? English people expect everyone to speak their language. I'm Sylvie, by the way."

"I'm Amal. You can add a little French to my language list as well. Would you like a piece of baklava?"

"No thank you, it's your lunch and I had a smörgås before I got on the tram. I just had to return here. Per, my boyfriend, later husband, brought me here for the first time fifty years ago. I have to admit I didn't think much of Prins Eugen's art collection, but the Park was just magical. I

64

hadn't seen red squirrels since I was a small child – never mind ones that ate out of your hand."

"The squirrels are still here. Fifty years ago, my father was here too – from Damascus. He was a microbiologist working on a research project."

"With the Wenner-Gren Institute?"

"Yes, but…"

"I was teaching in the International School here and some of my students had parents with the WG. I'm over now visiting my daughter, Maja. She's been working here for a year, but I've not been back since before she was born. Now, I'm catching up with her and wandering round my olden haunts."

"My sister-in-law was called Maja."

"It's an international name. When Per and I got married there was work for both of us in Oxford, so we made our home in England. When I got pregnant, we thought we would give our child a name that was Anglo-Swedish, but then we realized it would only work with a girl. Fortunately, that's what we got. Sten, Bo, Stig and especially, Rut and a boy would be given hell in an English school."

"Why's that?"

"In English, rut is what stags and reindeer do in the mating season."

"That's very funny, but I see what you mean. My lunch breaks aren't usually so entertaining. I'm the nurse here at the Palace gallery and I run a medical team who work in the museums on Djurgården."

"I'm glad you don't work with the art collection after what I said about it."

Amal's phone rang. "I agree with you though," she laughed, pulling the phone out of her bag. A quick glance at it and her expression changed. "Ursäkta mig, I must answer this. It's my nephew's school calling."

65

Sylvie watched as Amal listened and replied and guessed the news wasn't good.

"My nephew, Karim, is in trouble again. I have to go and see if I can change my shift. It was delightful talking to you."

Amal scooped up her lunchbox, threw it into her bag and hurried away.

The next day Sylvie was already in the gazebo, when Amal arrived.

"Sitta här," said Sylvie, patting the seat beside her, "and have some wienerbröd." She waved a box under Amal's nose. "I've got coffee too. Let's indulge in a little fika."

Amal sat down despondently and dipped into the box. "Tack."

"You're meant to look amazed and positively excited that an English person calls them Viennese pastries, not Danish," smiled Sylvie.

Amal looked confused.

"Forlåt. I'm so sorry. My mouth as usual gets carried away." Sylvie took a deep breath and speaking more softly moved nearer to Amal. "I'm meant to be cheering you up, but I'm just completely over the top. I've been to the Thielska Gallery this morning – better collection than here – but I couldn't stop thinking about how upset you looked yesterday, so I walked along the waterside from the café, in the hope you'd be here again. I'm just a nosy old lady and you don't have to share anything with me, but I'd like to help if I can."

"You're very kind, Sylvie and I'd like to talk with you."

Amal took a deep breath. "When my father left Stockholm and returned to Damascus, he met my mother, a nurse and they got married. Later my brother, Nabil was born and they hoped for another child. Fifteen years after my brother's birth, I arrived – Amal means 'hope'.

66

"My parents had always been international people. Some of our family branches are Muslim, some Christian, but to be honest, religion was never a major part of our lives and nor was politics. We just – how do you say it in English?... kept our heads down and got on with it.

"Eight years ago, the Wenner-Gren offered my brother a research opportunity. You cannot believe how proud that made my father. By then, Nabil was married to Maja and Karim was seven. You'll know what was happening in our country – the whole world does – and Nabil, desperate as he was to accept, was worried about leaving home. My father told him he'd never get another opportunity and that real life had to continue, so Nabil decided he would go unaccompanied for a couple of months and then send for Maja and Karim."

She paused. "So in spite of the turmoil Nabil left for Stockholm, but before his two months were up the hell the media called the Battle for Damascus descended on us. The short version is that I arrived back home after working nightmare hours at the hospital, to find our family house was destroyed... and the bodies of my parents and my sister-in-law in the ruins. I searched for Karim, but I couldn't find him. They eventually dug him out the next morning. He'd been trapped by his leg, but was still alive."

Sylvie gently broke the silence. "More coffee?"

"Tack." Amal took a long sip before continuing. "I was helped to contact my brother and the Swedes were fantastic. They got Karim and me out of Damascus, let us stay at the Wenner-Gren with my brother and they got Karim treatment for his leg. He will always have a limp and a scar on his face, but he's alive."

"You've gone through so much and..."

"There's more. Nabil decided to stay in Stockholm and continue his research. There was nothing in Syria for any

67

of us, so we were allowed to stay too. Less than six months after we'd arrived, Nabil had a heart attack – congenital, it turned out – and died too. It was just Karim and me. We couldn't live at the Wenner-Gren, but they helped us find somewhere to live and helped me find work.

"At first, Karim barely spoke and slept on the floor. If there was a loud noise, he cowered in the corner and then there were the nightmares. Gradually, he managed to function well enough to go to school where he didn't find it that difficult to learn Swedish, after learning English with my father like I had."

"So he has Arabic, English and Swedish too and he's – fifteen?"

"Yes, but now he's an angry teenager. Yesterday, he was talking to another student's sister and her brother told Karim he didn't want her talking to a scarfaced, murdering, Muslim bastard. It doesn't sound any better in Swedish. Then there was a fight."

"In the circumstances, you can hardly blame Karim. I hope the other lad was more severely punished then he was."

"I'm not sure about that, Sylvie. Karim's in school isolation today, then it's the weekend and on Monday, he has further isolation. The problem is that this isn't going to look good on his record and it's not the first time."

"I'd like to meet him, Amal. Would he talk to an old English lady?"

"He'll speak English with anyone. He loves the language even more than I do. That's part of his problem."

"Are you working tomorrow, Amal?"

"No, it's my weekend off."

"So, let's meet. I was planning on visiting the Vasa Museum, as fifty years ago the ship was a dripping hulk in the shipyard and I want to see the fancy modern museum where she lives now. You must have been a thousand times, but perhaps afterwards we could have lunch or…"

"Karim has only been to the Vasa once, when he was much younger, so we'd be happy to join you."

"Excellent. Outside the museum at 10.00?"

"We'll be there. Would your daughter like to join us?"

"She's… working this weekend. It'll just be the three of us."

"Good. He can be difficult."

"Don't worry. I was a teacher, remember and… there's a squirrel!"

"And this charming young man must be Karim. I'm very pleased to meet you," announced Sylvie, shaking Karim's hand vigorously. Scar or not, she thought, he's quite handsome. "Sylvie Bergström. That's Sylvie, as in 'wood' and Bergström, as in 'mountain stream'. I'm a little bit of the countryside in any language."

"Oh… I get it,' laughed Karim. "Amatty told me you were funny and loved words."

"I've had worse descriptions."

"Okay, English lady, I'm ready for you. Karim means 'generosity' and Halabi means 'from Aleppo', even though we come from Damascus."

"And here we all are in Stockholm admiring the wonderful design of this museum – a box? a ship? Either way, let's get in there quickly, a coach party's just arrived."

Karim lead the way into the dim interior and stopped abruptly.

"Look at those cannons. Not bad for a country that doesn't go to war." An elderly Swedish couple looked him up and down disdainfully and muttered to each other.

"She seems much larger than when I first saw her," said Sylvie loudly. "You couldn't get very near and she was so blackened and sodden there was no doubt she'd been sitting at the bottom of the sea for centuries. Now, she looks like a real warship, even if she did topple over after only twenty minutes afloat." She turned to Karim and whispered, "The cannons didn't help."

"But that twenty minutes and everything that followed, is why she's here four centuries later," said Amal. "Amazing."

"So do you only get into the history books, if something bad happens to you?" asked Karim. "That's not very fair."

"I think the most interesting finds," said Sylvie, steering Karim away from the ship's side to the display cases, "are the sailors and soldiers' personal belongings. Look at that boot – still laced up. It was probably the first time the owner had worn it."

"And he never took it off!" Karim, limped erratically towards the emergency exit. "Fan! Skuba mig inte!" he bellowed, barging through a crowd of Germans by the door.

"I'm so sorry, Amal, I didn't think. You go after him. I'll apologise to the Germans."

The Germans appeased, Sylvie found Amal and her nephew slumped outside on a waterside bench. "I'm sorry, Karim…"

"It's Karim who should be apologising to you, Sylvie" insisted Amal.

"I get angry a lot. I don't mean to. I remember things and everything falls apart. I'm sorry. Forlåt. Ana asif."

"You don't need to apologise to me, Karim; the word you needed was something like… Entschuldigung?

"Look, I can't imagine what you've been through. I'm the lucky English generation born after World War Two, for whom bombs falling and losing loved ones were memories trapped in our relatives' heads, not ours. In London, we were surrounded by bombsites where each

70

wallpapered rectangle and fireplace visible on the open walls, was a room a family had once lived in. My family's house was never hit, but my grandparents weren't so lucky. All through my childhood I wondered what would've happened to me, if I'd been born a couple of years earlier."

"I keep telling him, Sylvie, that we're the lucky ones too. We didn't have to trek overland; sail in leaky boats; fight through borders, or rot in camps. We arrived here by plane and train, like tourists, not refugees. We don't have to live in a neighbourhood with gangs, drugs and riots either."

"But that's what people see isn't it?" insisted Karim. "The world had never heard of Rinkeby until the riots. Then everyone knew they happened because of all those brown Muslim people the Swedes had let in. You know it's true, Sylvie. It wasn't like that fifty years ago, was it?"

"What I can see is that for a lot of immigrants, or refugees, their life here is many steps up from the life they left behind – but for you, it's steps down and that must be very difficult. I know it's easy for me to say, but you must climb up, keep climbing and show yourself and the Swedes what you can do."

Karim snorted. "I don't want to show the Swedes anything. I want to go to England. Can you help me?"

"You don't need my help. Just do your best in school and the rest will take care of itself. You're a clever young man, for goodness sake. Now enough of this. I need a coffee and cinnamon rush – so let's go and attack my favourite konditori on Sveavägen. All the problems of the world can be solved over a plate of cinnamon buns."

"What are you plans for tomorrow, Karim?" asked Sylvie later, when the kanelbullar seemed to have done their trick."

Karim shrugged.

"If you can stand another trip with me, I'd like to get

out of the city while the good weather lasts. A boat trip to the archipelago with a picnic lunch?"

"That's a lovely idea, Sylvie. Isn't it Karim?"

Karim nodded.

"I take that as a 'yes' then," said Sylvie getting to her feet. "I'll see you down on Strömkajen at 9.30 tomorrow. Hej då!"

"Have you ever been on Grinda before?" asked Sylvie, as the trio disembarked from the ferry.

"No, we've only been to Vaxholm," said Amal. "We've done quite a few tourist spots and then…"

"…realised we weren't tourists," added Karim.

"Grinda is a quieter island, where you can lose everyone else. Trees, rocks and water – one of my places. Let's find a pleasant little waterside spot and have our lunch."

"Over here," said Karim, five minutes later. "Enough trees, rocks and water for us, but no one else."

"Perfect," said Amal, kneeling down on the grass and opening a large canvas bag. "I've brought a few Syrian favourites. These are different kinds of falafel and these are sweet knafeh filo fingers with nuts and syrup."

"Delicious, Amal. There's such a fantastic variety of food here these days, but I've still brought the proper smörgåsar, kanelbullar and juice. I never picnic in England, but here I'd have a little red stuga summerhouse on my own rock, so I could live and eat outside all summer."

"But when winter comes," pointed out Karim, "you'd wish you were somewhere warmer."

"Nowhere's perfect, but look how clear the water is, even though there are boats using it."

Lunch finished, Amal curled up beside the picnic remains and fell asleep.

"She works hard to look after you, Karim."

"I know I worry her," he admitted.

"I wasn't sure which Karim would come today."

"What do you mean Sylvie?"

"Charming, clever, word-hungry Karim, or angry, rebellious, unthinking Karim. Do you know the English story, *Dr Jekyll and Mr Hyde*?"

"I know the story from a film."

"Other people see each of us differently – my daughter sees a totally different Sylvie from the one you see. Perhaps we should all have more than one name – but without murdering anybody. What's 'angry' in Arabic?"

"Ghadib."

"So are you Karim, or Ghadib?" asked Sylvie. "When you're Ghadib, think what Karim might do in the same circumstances. It might sound stupid, but stupid's what I do best, so think about it."

Karim smiled. "Well, Karim is heading for the water. Swimming's something the Swedes taught me and I enjoy it. I can move at the same speed as everyone else – sometimes even faster. I hope Ghadib, monster from the archipelago, does not… imerge? Emerge?"

"Emerge. Sounds like a good film title. I'm going to gently sunbathe over on that rock, before the season changes. Enjoy your swim."

Sylvie woke up to voices – agitated voices, shouting and crying. She clambered to her feet, but Amal was ahead of her slithering down the rocks.

Karim was dragging something out of the water and two women were shouting at him. Amal had reached them and was helping Karim to heave his burden on to the rocks. By the time Sylvie had climbed down there, Amal had already begun resuscitating a small body.

Karim had collapsed on to the ground.

"I'll call 112," Sylvie shouted scrambling back up the rocks.

By the time she had returned to announce the air ambulance was on its way, the child had regained consciousness.

"Are you all right, Karim? Whatever happened?"

"I was swimming back. To the shore," he gasped. "Something fell down off the rocks. A stone? A bird? Then I heard screams. Two women waving and shouting. Then I knew it was a person. I reached him. A frightened small child. He was so heavy. He struggled. I tried to keep his head... out of the water. Is he okay?"

"I think so. He's in your aunt's capable hands at the moment; the air ambulance is on its way and those Swedish ladies keep saying 'hjälte', which I think is 'hero'. Name number three?"

"A day out with you two," said Sylvie, an hour later, "is exhausting. One minute I'm peacefully snoozing, the next, you're both saving lives, a helicopter is hovering over my head and now courtesy of the Sjöpolisen, we're whizzing through the archipelago ruining what's left of my hair do! But why on earth didn't you want to go to the hospital Karim, or give your name to the child's mother?"

"I don't want any publicity," he snapped.

"Why not?"

"It would get twisted like everything else. The story would be I was drowning him, not rescuing him... or something stupid like that. We know what happened. His mother, aunt and the child know. That's all that matters."

"I think you're being very hard on yourself," said Amal.

"Maybe."

"Sylvie," said Amal, "our days out seem cut short with one thing or another, so please do come and have a meal with us next week. Friday evening? Here's my email. I'll send you the details."

"Thank you. I'd love to come."

74

To – amalhalabi@gmail.se 15.09.19 9.30

My Dear Friends,

I'm so sorry, but I'll not be able to join you on Friday. I'm flying back to England tomorrow. It's earlier than planned but something has come up which I need to attend to urgently.

I saw the article about the drowning child rescued by two mystery people. When the helicopter arrived I took a secret photo of you all, so if you ever decide you want Sweden to know it was you, I have the evidence.

I really enjoyed our time together.

Sylvie

~~~~~

To – sylviebergström@btinternet.co.uk 15.09.19 18.30

Dear Sylvie,

We are both so sad that you are leaving. We wish you a safe journey and we hope you will be back soon.

Karim says he will try and make sure that Ghadib does not emerge. Perhaps you know what that means?

Your friends,

Amal and Karim

~~~~~

To – amalhalabi @gmail.se 12.12.19 11.00

Dear Friends,

I am returning to Stockholm next week and I would love to meet up with you again.

Could we possibly meet at Skansen? It was the first Christmas market I ever saw and has such memories for me. Saturday 21st at 2.30 for the solstice sunset?

I can't wait to raise a glass of glögg to you both.

Sylvie

The dying rays of the midwinter sun were retreating across the snow, as Sylvie lifted the tray of glögg on to the table. "That's for you, Amal. Sorry, Karim, that's the non-alcoholic one, but the law's the law and that's mine." Swiftly she swapped her glass with Karim's. "Go on take a quick sip."

"That's good."

"Forlåt, that's your lot." She swapped the glasses back again and took a slow draught. "You're right. I'd forgotten how good that tastes. It's strange isn't it?" she said holding the glass up to the lamplight. "Take bog standard red wine. Slowly warm it with cinnamon, ginger, cardamom and orange. Drop raisins and almonds into your glass. Carefully pour the wine over them and it's transformed – midwinter in a glass."

She took another slow sip. "I've got something to tell you. I wasn't entirely honest when I was here last. I lectured Karim about being different people, when I'm no better. In fact, I'm worse – much worse. I left Stockholm early, because my daughter wanted me to leave. She wasn't working the weekend we went to Grinda, she was driving to her father's."

"Oh, I thought…"

"He was dead? I didn't exactly say that Amal, did I? The truth is I lead Maja to believe that, when all the time he was alive and living in Sweden."

"What?" Karim looked horrified. "How could you?"

"Sit down and let Sylvie explain, Karim."

"Because the Sylvie that did that was another person – a young single mum trying to do the best for her child. Per began having mental problems while I was pregnant. One minute life was perfect – it had taken a long time for me to conceive – and the next, our perfect life had collapsed around us. A distant cousin of Per's had been doing family research in the days before the internet did it for you and discovered that Per's grandfather, who Per knew had been an important civil servant during the war, was involved with the Baltic Repatriations."

"The what?" said Karim.

"At the beginning of the war, Latvians and Estonians were conscripted to fight in the Waffen-SS against the Soviet Union. By the end of the war, the Baltic countries were states of the Soviet Union and the Russians wanted back the Baltic soldiers who'd sought refuge in Sweden, so they could try them as traitors. Sweden kept the soldiers in detention camps and then handed them back to the Soviet Union, where they were all imprisoned and many of them were executed."

"But wasn't Sweden neutral then? It wasn't the soldiers' fault."

"Neutrality is not black and white, but shades of grey, Karim. There are still people who despise the Swedes for their war record. That's one of my less happy memories of fifty years ago.

"Per had idolised his grandfather – his grandparents had brought him up – and he couldn't believe that someone he'd loved so much was so different from the person he'd imagined him to be.

"Whatever the morality of the situation, it triggered something in Per. He kept muttering, 'Who am I?' over and over again and to cut a long, sad story short, he ended up in a mental hospital, just before our daughter was born. I called her Maja – the name we'd chosen together."

"That must have been dreadful for you," said Amal.

"It was very difficult, but what happened next was even worse. Per, supposedly, recovered and left the hospital, but he didn't come home to live with me and his newborn daughter. He went to recuperate," she stressed the word, "in Sweden. He didn't say goodbye, or unforgivably, set eyes on his daughter. He asked us to be out of the house when he collected his things and he would send for the rest. He wrote to tell me he wanted to start an entirely new life without us and to compensate for his grandfather. It turned out that Gwynneth, a nurse he'd met in the hospital, was part of that life and compensation. I didn't believe a word and that's the last I saw of him.

"Later, I quietly got a divorce. As soon as Maja was old enough to ask questions, I let her think he'd died in Sweden. I couldn't tell her anything else. Fortunately, I didn't have any relatives to tell her otherwise and we'd moved away from Oxford. Were there any photos of her with him? No, he'd been in Sweden when she was born prematurely and was involved in an accident, so he'd never returned.

"Maja was married, but she divorced two years ago. She wanted a change, decided she wanted to see her father's native land and applied for a job teaching here, like I did. Then she started researching her Swedish side of the family and I knew she was going to find out her father was alive, so I decided I had to tell her and I had to do it face to face, so over I came.

"I stupidly thought she'd think I'd made the right decision when she was a baby. But she didn't. She'd found a Swedish relative online who'd never met her father, but was sure he could find out where Per lived – and he did.

"Coming back to Stockholm, brought back a lot of memories for me and on the day I met you, Amal, I thought I would begin retracing my steps to try and remember Per, as he was then – as we were then – and then share those moments with Maja. I went through a total charade of trying to become the person I was then. But when you told me your family's story, I was so ashamed of what I'd done, I had to help you instead."

Karim looked up. "I still can't believe you acted like you did that weekend, knowing where your daughter was."

"I can't believe it either. I was the monster from the archipelago and you were the hero.

"That weekend, Maja drove all the way up to Umeå without telling her father she was coming. She found the house and saw there was some kind of celebration outside in the garden – adults, children, babies – but she couldn't get out of the car. Those people would never be her family and she knew it. She drove straight back and was so exhausted and upset, she couldn't bear to have me in the house.

"Then a month ago, she got in touch and said she was sorry. She'd been thinking it through, over and over again and decided that she'd have done exactly the same as I'd done, if she'd been in my shoes. Then she asked me to come back over and hoped we could travel back to England together, for Christmas and New Year."

"But that's wonderful, Sylvie. Why didn't you bring Maja this afternoon?"

"She's setting up for a party at the school. That's the truth.

"Now, Karim we need to get down to business. Maja teaches in the same school I taught in and I was there yesterday. I've been in touch with them since I left in September. They've just set up a programme of special scholarships for students aged sixteen, so they can study for the International Baccalaureate. They particularly favour students with good language skills, as study is in English with other languages.

"I told the Principal about you, Karim. I just happened to have a photo of you. Just the one. I told him I would like to recommend you for a scholarship beginning next September. You would have to work hard in your current school this year, but I know you could do it and end up with a wonderful career – in whatever language, or whatever country you wanted. What does Karim," she stressed his name, "think?"

"Say something, Karim," pleaded Amal.

"I'm speechless. Karim... Karim thinks that he'd love that, Sylvie. You're so generous."

"You are too, Karim. Remember, that's the first thing you told me when we met and don't let's forget this," she said pulling a tiny Swedish flag out of the table decorations, "The lines of gold in the Nordic cross signify generosity. It's never too late, whoever you are; whatever you've done; whatever's been done to you, to move on – with generosity."

"Maja and I would like to invite you to lunch tomorrow. She can tell you more about the school and all the opportunities that are available there."

"I can't believe it," said Karim, getting to his feet. "I promise I'll not let you and your daughter down. Back in one minute." He limped off into the maze of crowded stalls.

"We can't thank you enough, Sylvie," said Amal.

"You've helped me more than you know and Karim can help me even more by getting that scholarship."

"Did I hear my name mentioned again? There you are ladies, more glögg and of course," he said sliding the plate towards Sylvie, "warm kanelbullar, just in case there are more problems that need solving this afternoon."

He raised his glass, "God Jul och..."

"Skål!"

About the author

Margaret Bulleyment began writing fiction and plays, after a long career in comparative education. She has had short stories published in anthologies, including Bridge House's *CaféLit*; *Snowflakes*; *Baubles; Glit-er-ary; Crackers; Nativity* and on story websites.

As a finalist in the Ovation Theatre Awards, she has twice had short plays performed professionally. Her children's play *Caribbean Calypso* was runner-up in Trinity College of Music and Drama's 2011 International Playwriting Competition and is available on TreePress. In December 2017, the play was performed three times in Bangalore, India by Jagriti Kids – a charity promoting literacy and school attendance.

Making a Decision

Dawn DeBraal

After two years of dodging it, Verna Mae Peal was hosting her first Ladies Historical Society Luncheon. All twenty-five members of the Society had served a luncheon in their homes, except for Verna Mae. It was something she ignored until she could no longer avoid it. It was her turn to host.

Verna Mae cleaned her house twice, being taught that her home reflected directly upon her. The menu decision had been a nightmare, she couldn't decide, so her caterer suggested the menu while her baker decided the dessert.

All of her life, Verna Mae was incapable of making a decision. She let her parents pick her husband, and Darrell made all the decisions for them. Verna Mae meekly went along with everything because it was more comfortable that way. After Darrell left for work, she called her sister about hosting the luncheon.

"What do I wear?"

"The new dress we picked out!" her sister Laura told her.

Verna Mae pulled the sundress out of her closet. She set up her good china service for twenty-five, buffed the crystal glasses polished the silverware, styling her hair the way her hairstylist suggested. She looked in the mirror, hoping her efforts were good enough. The first guest arrived at eleven-thirty. Verna Mae opened the door to Coretta Dumfries.

"Please come in! Make yourself at home. May I serve you a refreshment?" Verna Mae said brightly. Coretta was half an hour early.

"Sorry," Coretta pulled her body up the steps. "I'm early. I just don't get around like I used to. I never know how long it will take me to get somewhere."

"Mama always said the early bird gets the worm!" Verna Mae said brightly.

"When you get old like me, you have to get there, especially early! How can I help?" Coretta offered. Verna Mae didn't know what to say. Coretta suggested she lay out the napkins. Verna had already done this, three times but she wanted Coretta to feel useful. The ladies started to arrive.

"Verna Mae, you have a beautiful house, so clean!" Annabelle told her.

"My mama always says a clean house is a Godly house."

"Your landscaping is beautiful!"

"I have a wonderful gardener," Verna Mae responded. Sofie Atwell arrived. Verna Mae let her in.

"I love your hair!"

"My hairstylist picked the style and cut I just couldn't decide. She told me, 'Verna Mae, this is what you should have.' "

Two by two the ladies came, all of them anxious to see what they'd been missing over the past two years.

"These are beautiful flowers!"

"My florist did an excellent job picking out heirloom flowers for me. This is the historical luncheon after all."

"Verna Mae, I love your china!" said another.

"Thank you. It was my Grandma Birdie's china. Darrell and I were going to pick something out when we got married, but my grandma passed away. Mama said I should just take Grandma Birdie's set."

"That's a pretty dress!"

"Thank you, my sister, Laura, helped me pick it out at Carson's Store." Verna Mae felt she was doing fine with the party. The ladies had been served their refreshments and sat chatting. Coretta reminded the ladies that after the luncheon, they would begin their meeting, thanking Verna Mae for hosting this month's party. Everyone applauded, saying how beautiful things were. Verna Mae glowed as she excused herself to set out the sandwiches and assorted salads suggested to her by her caterer for the greatest ease in preparation and presentation.

The ladies filed around the table, serving themselves on Grandma Birdie's china and silverware. Verna Mae started to relax when she realized that the worst of the hosting was over. The ladies seemed to be enjoying themselves. After the clean-up, Coretta started the meeting. Verna Mae was shocked when she heard the front door open. Coming into the foyer, she found her disgruntled husband, Darrell, standing there.

"There's no place to park!" he hissed.

"Darrell, honey, I told you about the Historical Luncheon today. Did you forget?"

"What? They are still here? I need some supper. It's my poker night tonight. Send them packing now."

"Darrell, I can't do that; it's my turn to host!"

Darrell stared at his wife. "I want my supper. How much longer?"

Verna Mae stepped back a little. "I don't know exactly, honey. I'll get them moving. Why don't you go upstairs and take a shower? I'll see what I can do,"

Verna Mae could feel the panic rising in her body. Sweat tinged her upper lip. The ladies were only on the third agenda item. She didn't know what to say. How could she tell the ladies that her husband wanted them gone, just when things were going so well?

Coretta, who was running the meeting started to cough uncontrollably.

"Annabelle will finish with the treasury report. I am going to get a glass of water. Please, excuse me." Coretta made her way to the kitchen. Verna Mae was already standing there, handing her a glass of water.

"I don't need any water; it was just an excuse. What's wrong?" Coretta looked at Verna Mae, empathetically. She took the glass of water from her and put it down on the countertop.

"It's Darrell. He's home. He wants his supper. He has a poker game tonight. I sent him up to take a shower. I just don't know what to do." Verna Mae wrung her hands.

Coretta put her hands around Verna Mae's. "Make him a bologna sandwich," Coretta said quietly.

"But Darrell hates bologna!" said Verna Mae.

"So what?" Coretta winked at her taking a sip of the water and walked back out to the meeting.

Verna Mae made a bologna sandwich, adding celery and carrot sticks to the bag. Darrell came downstairs; his hair still wet from the shower.

"What are they still doing here? I told you to get rid of them!"

Verna Mae handed Darrell the sandwich.

"What's this?" Darrell took the bag.

"That's your supper." Verna Mae smiled at her husband charmingly.

"My supper! What is it?"

"A bologna sandwich,"

"I hate bologna," Darrell said disgustedly.

"That's supper, or at least what I am prepared to make you for supper tonight." Verna Mae answered. She stood firm pursing her lips one arm folded over the other, daring her husband to say one more word about it. Darrell grabbed the sandwich out of her hand, turning on his heel.

"I can't believe you'd give your husband a bologna sandwich for his dinner,"

Verna Mae opened the front door motioning for Darrell to leave.

"Verna Mae, this is my house." Darrell sputtered.

85

"This is my house too Darrell, remember my parents bought it for us?" She waved him out the door.

Coretta paused her report when she saw Darrell's car leave the neighbourhood at an accelerated rate of speed.

Verna Mae was a quick study. She didn't even have to mull it over. For once in her life Verna Mae had made a decision, all on her own.

About the author

Dawn DeBraal lives in rural Wisconsin with her husband Red, along with a slightly overweight rat terrier and a cat. She has discovered a love for telling a good story. Her works have been published in several online magazines and anthologies. She loves writing short stories, poems, and songs.

www.amazon.com/Dawn-DeBraal/e/B07STL8DLX

Malak al Mawt

Steve Wade

Alone. Utterly alone. All my family had gone the way of countless others. Not just like those in my home country, but throughout the globe. My young wife went first. Taken from me through the slaying hands of another man; a man with righteousness in his heart and hatred in his soul. A man affected by delusion. One who seemed to believe that the radioactive contamination with which my wife was riddled was contagious.

I came upon him, this lady-slayer, as he straightened from his terrible deed. Just paces from where my family and I had holed up in a temporary refuge. His killing hands red and slick with my wife's lifeblood. Both of us as startled as the other, he had the advantage of a killer in killing mode. He came at me like a panther, his eyes wide and maddened. And then a sheet of white flashed across my vision. While the ground came up to meet me. He'd hit me. Through blurred images I watched him bear down upon me. Another white-hot flash. And then nothing.

When I came to, it took me a few seconds to separate what I couldn't be sure belonged to the agitated state of half-sleep and reality. But my wife's empty and stricken shell lying next to me revealed the horrific truth. Already the scavengers had begun to feed. I threw back my head from where I lay and tried to scream out. But my larynx was empty. I screamed again the silent scream of a helpless movie-victim trapped in a haunted castle.

I brought my hand to my head where my wife's killer had hit me. Where he'd rained his blows upon me and left me too for dead. I worked my splayed fingers about my scalp, but felt no injuries or bumps. I looked at my bloodless fingertips, and felt my head again. No blood. So strange. But the face of the man who had butchered my wife forming in my mind's eye overcame my unfocused curiosity: A bearded man, as pale as sun-bleached bones. As emaciated as a diseased rat. The alpha male, I had heard about, in a pack of human rats that had set themselves up as a cleansing squad. To clean up the city by ridding it of the contaminated. A man I vowed to track down and annihilate. The reason I went on when all purpose, all meaning, had ended.

And then two of the remaining parts of that purpose, my three children, were taken from me through starvation. I, as their father, had done my best to scour the poisoned streets for anything that might keep their sick and malnourished bodies alive: an overlooked tin of beans in a store that had been looted countless times. Noodles, packet soup, coffee, powdered milk, apple chips, dried figs, whatever I might find. And all or any of the other things that had been stockpiled or hoarded since the experts first indicated the warning signs. But I failed.

I needed something, someone to blame for my loss and failure. This I mulled over for some time, until the answer, like an unwelcome anthropoid, virus-ridden and ailing, came club-footedly limping into my thoughts: The bearded man, my wife's killer. In killing her he had annihilated the possibility of any future children we may have had together. Not that these unborn children could have ever replaced the ones we lost. But, in time, if the world reverted to normal, got over its latest malady as it had others throughout its history, the new children would have given us a focus – something on which to devote our broken lives.

The streets were filled with a myriad of scavenging bodies maddened by the same hunger to feed themselves and their kin. I endured blows, vile tongues, and cowardly attacks from behind. I wiped from my face the pungent stink of other men's spittle. But I fought back. With what little strength I had left in my own weakened body, I struck out. I roared profanities into stranger's faces. I drew blood, broke bones and maimed. I may have ended the lives of some. I'm not sure. I never stopped to check. And I don't care.

And then came the evening when I returned home to the underground storage tank in the derelict filling station. The den where I'd tried to keep my children safe. Where the last of my three boys, the eldest, had held on to life weeks after the two younger ones had succumbed to the hunger and the Baltic cold.

But there he was. No. Not him. His lifeless body. No more the one-time smiling boy. The boy whose smiles had made his mother weep. Whose piping voice calling out 'Daddy' pierced my chest and left me breathless. Those smiles ended now, that little voice silenced. Over. Just nine years old. And a lad of nine years he would remain forever.

I fell to my knees, oblivious to the shards of broken glass puncturing my legs. I picked up his little body and cradled it to my chest. And there I remained until the last of the warmth drained from him. By then the freezing cold had penetrated me to the marrow. My body shook uncontrollably. Not just because of the Arctic cold, but with shock and horror.

Burying my boy wasn't easy. Even though I concealed his body by wrapping it in an old sack cloth we had used as a blanket, the vagabonds of the streets trailed me like a colony of vultures. And then others saw the vultures circling. Citizens who were not natural born killers, but induced predators. Men and women who were once ordinary and law-abiding. But they too shifted into killing mode. Or at least scavenging mode. Although they would have slaughtered me to get to my dead child. For them, not a child, but a carcase they could feed upon. That would allow them to survive until the next meal.

But I countered any impromptu prey rush. The lead vultures were weak and scrawny. And I had the strength of a father's guilt and love to fuel my defence. A carpenter when times were normal, I had fashioned a fighting staff from a branch taken from a red oak tree before all the oaks and other plants were diseased or dead. And I carried with me an assassin dagger. From my martial arts club. The tip of the dagger's blade, a blade with which I sliced open their arms and outstretched hands, plunged with ease into their bellies. And I felt the instant hotness of their poisonous blood on my hands and wrists.

The trailing vagabonds, like a cackle of haranguing hyenas, turned tail. Even in the sight and scent of nourishment, their miserable lives were worth more to them than the risk standing between them and the meal that would ensure their survival. But, like all wily scavengers, they took after me again, but at a safe distance.

But my tenacity outweighed their hunger. My own appetite had disappeared. I no longer craved sustenance. Nor did it occur to me to think about food. Not till later. And even then it was more a curiosity as to why my appetite had disappeared.

This wasn't the case for the thousands that thronged the streets. Like packs of starved and sickly curs, they trotted, limped and dragged themselves about. Many of them sightless, their retinas burned away by the flash of the nuclear explosion. Their faces devoid of fellowship and good will, as they sniffed and searched among the festering rubbish for anything edible.

For those animals and plants that survived the blast, the fallout left them diseased, contaminated, stunted or dying.

All except one creature, it seemed. A blue roan stallion that had wandered in from the burnt and parched countryside soon after the flash of light that lit up the night sky and made it bleed. Something about this animal kept the famished mobs from falling upon it as they had other straying beasts and birds. And this had nothing to do with concerns for their health and safety. They had gone beyond caring. As evidenced in the way they fell upon and fed on anything dead or dying, animal or human.

Perhaps it had to do with the stallion's vitality when pitted against the infected living, the almost dead. Its eyes, as red as unbridled hatred, burned fiercely. Those eyes were almond-shaped, like those of a wolf.

With ears pointed forward, the stallion ignored the cowardly fleeing, snorted, and fixed those crimson eyes on me. I returned its intense gaze. The stallion bowed its head and clomped towards me. I knew then that it knew that I knew.

It stopped before me. I raised a hand and grasped its reins. My other hand I placed upon its muzzle. That's when a jolt flashed through my head. Like being struck maybe by its back hooves. But in the aftermath of that jolt, images formed in my head of a place I had, to my knowledge, never before seen. On the shores of a silvery bay in the blue shadow cast by a mountain, there stood a sturdy castle with a single turret. And in the foreground of the castle, on the edge of the bay, a silhouetted figure swinging from a gallows.

Unable, it seemed, to pull my hand away from the stallion's muzzle, the creature jerked its head upwards and I collapsed to the ground. Never before had I felt so completely drained. Not only of energy, but of life. This, I felt, must be what it feels like to die. Or perhaps I was dying. So there I lay and awaited death. But death did not come.

In place of death, a high nickering from the blue roan beast. This pervaded my being. I worked my way to my feet. In me now a sudden fire that suffused me with a sense of invincibility. The stallion snorted and he pawed the earth with one leg stretched forward. And, as though he and I had been in partnership forever, I leaped atop his back and clutched his reins.

The stallion reared upwards, its front legs pounding the air like a professional boxer. Then off we went to I knew exactly where. Through the cloying streets we galloped, the masses giving way, while the helpless, from doorways and gutters, just stared through hopeless eyes. Too weak some of them to even turn their heads, their eyes shifted like the liquid in a spirit level. But when we came upon men engaged in what was obviously a cleansing operation, the fiery stallion and I shifted course as though as one.

They were operating in of six to eight. Those members of the rat-pack that survived the stallion's killing hooves, I finished off with my red oak staff. We came upon one particular squad in an alleyway too narrow for a truck to pass through. The dying screams of the victims drew us to them. But the screams of the cowardly killers as we ran them down and caved in their skulls with staff and hooves lessened the agonised screams of the innocent as they lay dying.

On we galloped. Out of the city and into the countryside, where the destruction caused by nuclear fallout was starker still. The land was parched and blackened. A sulphuric stench shifting on the wind. What grass cover was left lay yellow and dried up. While copses of alder, ash and aspen rattled like skeleton drudges. And lone tree skeletons stood out in stark silhouettes. While scattered about the barren fields and lying in the ditches, the skin and bone carcasses of cattle, sheep and horses. Others newly dead and bloated like beached whales. And there were the scorched bodies of people too. Dotted about. Some lay lifeless where they had been tending their crops when the explosion struck.

To mask the heavy stench, I pulled my hood across my face, which covered my nose and mouth. On we galloped through what may have been night and day. I couldn't tell as daylight and night seemed to have melded together to form a permanent state of semi-darkness.

At what could have passed for daybreak, we came to the place I had seen when I first placed my hand upon the stallion: The castle beneath the mountain next to the sea. A place I had never before beheld but now knew I had known always.

But then I heard a wondrous sound. From the skies above the bay – shrieking seabirds – gulls and kittiwakes. I twisted about in the saddle, as did the stallion on which I sat, his ears pointed forward in the direction of a flock of gannets that dived headfirst at terrible speed into the water. A school of porpoises broke the surface – three of them.

The melodic trilling of songbirds coming from inland turned my attention back to the castle and its surroundings. I recognised the song of the wren and blackbird, but there were others I couldn't identify. What I did understand was that here was a place unaffected, untouched maybe, by nuclear attack or fallout.

I inhaled deeply the sweet scent of grass shifting to the saltiness of the sea. I licked the salt from my lips. And saw that the sun was indeed rising. And as it rose, it gilded the land in a golden light that pointed up the greenness of the grass and the vibrancy of the russet reds and browns of the hilly countryside.

The snorting of the stallion turned my attention to a lone figure, his head bowed, walking along the shoreline. I tugged on the stallion's reins and we rode towards him, though without speed.

As I neared him I felt as much saw who he was. The bearded man who had taken from me my wife. But I surprised myself with my own calmness. And although he clearly heard us arriving, he only looked up when I stopped before him.

"I've been expecting you," he said.

Curious now as to why he had been expecting me, I lowered my red oak staff. "Go on," I said.

He explained that sometimes the sick and injured reach a stage where there is nothing left but the inevitable. And that to keep them alive is to prolong their suffering. "Everything must one day die," he said. "Even Death."

I felt as though he was trying to convince me that his slaying of my wife was a mercy killing.

"Who are you?" I said.

"You might well ask the same question of yourself," he said.

"I have no time for riddles or philosophy." I raised my staff above my head.

On his face a look of acceptance, but he held up his right palm as if to ask my pardon and grant him a final word. To hear him out before he met his inevitable fate. I relaxed the grip on my staff.

"Look," he said, indicating the still surface of a rocky pool.

I dismounted and walked to the pool. Ensuring I kept him at a distance and at my right side and in my periphery. I looked.

"What do you see?" he said.

"Nothing," I said, shaking my head.

"Exactly," he said. And he came to the edge of the pool next to me. "Death has no reflection."

"You mean?"

He nodded. But no reflected figure nodded back from the water's surface.

94

With the blue roan stallion standing stock still on the beach behind us, the bearded man and I set about gathering driftwood. Together we dug a hole and stood a large beam upright into the sand, strengthening it with small boulders and rocks. Before covering the rocks with sand and tamping it down. We then secured a cross beam at its top. And finally we found some old fisherman's rope and fashioned this into a hang noose, which we attached to the crossbeam.

That's when I whistled to the stallion. He came to us. And the bearded man, on the chucking of my chin, clambered atop the beast whose eyes were now flaring as red as they had been when I first saw him. The man kicked his heels into the stallion's flanks. The beast walked forward and beneath the gallows. I then placed the rope about the bearded man's neck. Tightened it and tapped the stallion's rump. He moved forward and left the bearded man dangling.

I then swung myself back into the saddle and moved up the beach and watched until the hanging man's body stopped quivering.

From the castle I watched and listened to the hordes of men, foot-soldiers, ready to follow their new leader, me, back into the realm of the living. The Soldiers of Mercy, and at the helm, Death: the new Death.

About the author

Steve Wade's short fiction has been widely published and anthologised. He has had stories shortlisted for the Francis McManus Short Story Competition and for the Hennessy Award. His stories have appeared in over fifty print publications, including Bridge House Publishing, who have also published his short story collection: *In Fields of Butterfly Flames and Other Stories*, He has won First Prize in the Delvin Garradrimna Short Story Competition on four occasions.

www.stephenwade.ie

Marry in Blue

C L Spillard

"So: do you believe in Climate Change, then?" His tone mocked.

Louise took a slight step back. "That's a bit of an…" She adjusted the crystal flute in her hand, "Unusual way of putting it." She studied the bubbles.

"Believe. I mean, do you believe I'm standing here right in front of you, holding a glass of…"

What if it was more than just Prosecco? What if someone had put something in it? And what if that explained her total inability – try as she might, all afternoon – to get into a stress-free conversation with anyone from the groom's side of the guest-list…?

"Oh look, they're cutting the cake."

She made her way over to the back of the marquee, careful on soft grass in heels higher than she'd worn for months.

Tyler, dressed in a suit she thought a little too sharp, towered over Tess, who still had on her green gown from the ceremony.

Marry in green: shame to be seen.

The two looked awkward together. Tyler's dark shaggy curls had a personality clash with the geometry of his suit, and neither complemented Tess's gown or her golden halo of hair.

Louise chafed at the lack of a chance to chat with either. Perhaps she shouldn't have bothered coming. She hardly knew their Local Branch Chair Tess, she'd never heard of Tyler until the gold-edged invitation card had arrived, and she had only one dress – blue peasant-style with unfashionable puffed sleeves – that still fitted her.

But then it appeared everyone in Local Branch had been invited, there'd be dancing, and if it all turned out to be a bit much she'd only be a short walk from her pleasingly shabby attic flat behind the graceful tiered curve of the Royal Crescent.

Everybody cheered: the knife had come away clean.

They moved to take their seats at crisp, round tables. After she'd found her name on its decorative card and taken her place, men she didn't know sat either side of her. The one to her left, she noticed, wore a clumsy square ring on his right-hand middle finger.

"Been to any good protests lately?"

"Er…"

The starter arrived, and with it the guilt.

Tess's attitude to those in Local Branch who hadn't changed to a vegan diet had become, as Louise liked to put it so as not to upset anybody, "a bit of a talking point" – a talking point about which she'd rather not, actually, talk.

"Are you vegan?"

"No, I'm not. I had to-"

"Why not?"

After the afternoon's string of strained conversations she finally snapped. "Doctor's orders. I'm anaemic."

She watched him start to shovel the tofu salad into his mouth before she leaned in and whispered, "Heavy periods."

He stopped shovelling.

Dry sparks shot across her hands.

People would say, "That's not like you."

She turned her attention to her companion to the right, whose plate already lay clean.

"Would you like my starter? I…"

She'd known in advance she wouldn't be able to eat much.

"Aye, go on love. Pity to waste it."

They swapped plates.

"Smile!"

With the camera on her, she picked up her glass to cheer. Her companion did the same.

"God's Own County!"

She warmed to the main course – a comforting bean casserole – and to her Yorkshire neighbour. "Where're you from?"

"Otley. Ruddy frackers. Did you know, they're right in our National Park now?"

"Yes, I've been following it on the News," she said. "My mum's been to the protest camp there. She took them some food."

His blunt expression about where the fracking firm could go finally brought the relief of a laugh.

Until she realised he'd named the wrong firm.

She turned away.

She must keep calm.

She'd had three glasses and she might be letting her imagination run away with her.

MI5 did this sort of thing. She'd read about it in the paper: people getting a whole false identity and infiltrating protest groups.

It would explain everything.

Everything except this: *who were all Tyler's wedding guests*? There must be nearly fifty of them. There couldn't be fifty people who'd had to disappear and start a whole new life just for this, surely?

Her hand shook as she poured herself a tumbler of water.

When she turned back, her Yorkshire neighbour had disappeared. But his jacket kept watch, in his place.

She glanced around – saw everybody deep in conversation.

98

She shouldn't really do this. And how embarrassing if someone were to notice!

She devised an excuse in advance: *He'd dropped it.*

She folded her left arm across her middle – extended her hand to the lapel, the chair-back; the inner breast pocket.

A wallet. And a pen: she'd brought no bag; just put her door keys in a tiny pocket.

She found a name, a firm; an address.

She wrote with shaking hands, holding the white napkin on her knees.

She couldn't bring herself to eat her dessert so she swapped it with the starter man, who seemed to have regained his prodigious appetite. When he got up to get more drink he lurched and knocked his chair over.

She watched him make his way past where the band had started tuning up and seized her chance – stole her second name and address from a driving licence as she righted the chair.

People had begun to get up from the tables to mingle. But her napkin wouldn't fit in the pocket with her keys! She was stuck. Damned dresses and their tiny pockets.

Damned dresses... she smiled – recalled the last time she'd worn this one.

Walking back home in the dusk one evening in the spring, through this very park in fact, she had crossed through a group on one of the town's 'Ghost Walks'. As the stragglers meandered past her and they exchanged nods and smiles, she overheard their guide round off his tale with the words: "... and her ghost walks this path, wearing a blue dress."

Everybody had looked round.

"Louise!"

She turned.

Tess smiled down at her.

She folded the incriminating napkin, stuffed it into a puffed sleeve and clipped the pen to the tight elastic.

"Glad you could make it. Will said you hadn't been well."

"Oh that was *ages* ago. I'm better now."

Being mistaken for a ghost, even in jest, had been the final straw. She'd gone for help the very next day.

"What was it?"

"I had… well I just needed supplements."

And to eat more: give up being vegan…

Her face felt hot: her hands cold.

"So: what d'you think of Tyler, then?"

"I haven't really had a chance to… er…" She brightened. "How did you two meet, anyway?"

She noticed Tess glance sideways.

The band struck up. Tyler came over and conducted his bride to the dance floor. Louise studied the chair where he'd been sitting.

The dancing made wallflowers of the handbags just as the bar had made widows of the jackets. Coloured spotlights stole into the fading day. In the darkening spaces between, Louise warmed to her self-appointed mission.

Between steals she danced. It burned away her doubts, her guilt and three glasses of Prosecco. By eight she was ready to head for home.

As she finished saying her goodbyes to Tess and Tyler, someone tapped her on the shoulder.

"Will!"

"Thought I'd show my face."

"I'm just going. I'm a bit worn-out."

She hesitated – wanted him to say something…

"Before you disappear – can I come round tomorrow morning with the Newsletters?"

"Oh yes. Yes, no problem. About eleven? Then I can do my round in the afternoon."

Was that the door intercom?

Louise sat up in bed and looked for the time. Quarter to eleven. She pulled on her dressing-gown and went through to the kitchen to buzz Will in, before putting the kettle on.

When she heard footsteps up the last flight of stairs she opened the door.

Tyler stood there.

He had running gear on.

She balked: looked him up and down.

Thank God she'd had the presence of mind to lock the napkins in her desk drawer last night, even if she'd not got round to her search.

"Can I come in?"

His voice, his whole aspect, took her aback: softer than she'd expected.

She didn't want to slam the door on his fingers.

She let him walk through. "I thought... thought you two were setting off today."

"No, it's the day after tomorrow."

"Oh." She didn't know what else to say.

"Tess's passport didn't come through in time to book the flight—"

"You're *flying*?" Her eyes widened.

"Her idea."

"*Hers*?" She glared.

The intercom buzzed.

What now?

She'd have to let Will in.

He wouldn't know who else was here.

He'd be carrying the names and addresses of every

101

member of Local Branch, on those newsletters. The only one who kept those names: his idea. In case…

She got up – hesitated.

She crossed the kitchen…

Picked up the handset…

Wished Will could speak Hungarian, like her flatmate Mike who was learning it from his girlfriend.

She listened for his voice. Yes, that was Will.

"Hi! Tyler's dropped round."

But he wouldn't know what she meant…

She pressed the buzzer. "Come up!"

She rushed to the door. "Come in!"

She wrenched the bundle of papers from his hands and bolted to the bedroom, calling over her shoulder, "Just go through to the kitchen: I've made tea…"

She unlocked the desk drawer and shoved the newsletters in with the napkins. She locked the drawer and pocketed the key.

Tyler wasn't going anywhere. He'd sat down with Will at the kitchen table, and they'd fallen to swapping tales about running.

"I've got to get dressed. I'm going out shortly."

That should work.

But when she returned, ten whole minutes later, neither had budged.

Tyler stared right at her. "I saw what you were doing yesterday."

She might be sick.

"I came to thank you."

"Sorry?" She struggled for words. "What… for?"

He pulled out a chair for her to sit. "How much do you know about my family?"

"Nothing." She hesitated. "Er – yet." She took the chair. At least he wouldn't see her legs shaking.

"Well, when you do, you'll find out we're a military family. Generations of us."

That made sense.

Will sat bolt upright.

She noticed him glance in the direction of the bedroom. "Including me."

Something drew her eyes to the window. Third floor. Would he do them both in and make it look like an accident? Because he knew she'd found out who he was – what he was doing?

Don't be daft.

"Just training. I went through with it. So I could do what I do now."

"What-"

"I was on that truck that got impounded in Malaysia."

"Blimey!" She and Will exchanged glances.

The arrests at the logging protest had been all over the news last year.

Prove it.

"I've got Channel 4's footage if you ever want to know for sure."

She realised she'd been glaring at him.

He pulled out his phone – scrolled through a list.

"This is from Tess's phone. I'd not noticed before, it's a forces' issue one, massively encrypted. But I know how to hack into the system. I downloaded this last night."

He stopped on a page.

"I only thought to have a listen because I noticed you yesterday, sifting through all our things. Looking *suspicious* – sorry."

He laid the phone flat on the table.

"Good job too. Listen to this."

Tess's voice came, clear as a bell.

She sounded smug.

She addressed the other person as 'Blue'.

She was 'pleased to report' she'd 'disrupted' Local Branch.

And now, as briefed, she'd 'infiltrated Headquarters'.

About the author

C.L. Spillard is a complex interplay of matter and energy in a wave-pattern whose probability cloud is densest in York.

The moon landings influenced the young pattern's self-awareness mechanisms, igniting a lifelong interest in physics and humanity's plight on Earth.

C.L. Spillard claims responsibility for several published short stories, the fantasy novel *The Price of Time*, and its sequel *The Evening Lands*, published by Rhetoric Askew.

www.cspillardwriter.co.uk

Me and the Bird

Penny Rogers

I can see it hopping up and down in that glittering cage. It looks like a peacock from here, but they're quite big so it must be something else. How big are pheasants? Anyway, it doesn't matter. I won't be able to get over this bridge to see it properly or to let it go; the bridge is too steep, too long, and much too dangerous.

So why do I keep trying? Well I don't. It's just this stupid dream; I've been having it ever since the accident. Right now, even when I'm awake I think about the bird. It's always there, going round and round in my mind. Shall I? Shan't I? Most nights I dream about it. Sometimes the dream goes away. Once it went away for a few weeks. But just when I thought it had gone for good it came back. Now that wretched bird is in my mind the whole time; I dream about it when I'm asleep, I think about it when I'm awake.

To get to the bird I've got to get over a bridge, so steep it's almost perpendicular. I think it's one of those old ones built to let tall ships through. Sometimes I'm struggling up that steep bit, and I know there's no way I'm going to get across to get close to the bird, so I give up worrying about it. It's all so tiring. Even though I'm asleep I feel exhausted; I've got enough to worry about without adding fabulous birds to the list.

Other times I seem to be able to have some control over the dream. I can make sure that things I've got to carry are properly packed, for example, or that I've left the kids with their dad, or that my mum is safe at home. It doesn't mean that I cross the bridge though; something always goes wrong. Once I remember getting to the top and seeing my friend on a boat sailing underneath. I called to her, but she didn't hear so I shouted and shouted; she still didn't hear and I woke up yelling to her.

I don't feel sorry for the bird. In the real world I hate the idea of keeping birds in cages and this pheasant, or whatever it is, is clearly too big for the little space it lives in. Mind you, it's a very upmarket cage, all gold with jewels around the top and bottom. It looks Moroccan, gold and blue, the colours of the sun, the sky and the sea. And I can see diamonds, ice diamonds sparkling like the sun on alpine snow, my nemesis.

Although I don't feel sorry for the bird, I would like to let it out; I'd be interested to see if it could fly. That could be difficult though, watching it fly when I can't walk anymore.

Sometimes the bridge is booby-trapped. Really it is. Just when I'm doing well, marching along, singing, swinging my arms – I can still do those sorts of things in my dream – I fall over. Smack onto my face or crash down onto my arse. Someone digs holes and covers them up, like elephant traps, so I don't see them until I've fallen. The funny thing is, when this happens I wake up in agony, like after the accident. Once I walked straight into a wire stretched across the bridge, about five feet from the ground. It really hurt my neck.

The worst bit is going down on the far side. It's a terrifying descent, very steep, and to make things worse the bridge is broken and the bricks and mortar have been replaced by some sort of ladder. I can't walk across it; I have to crawl, all the while trying not to look down at the water far below me. It's so easy to slip, it happens so fast and I can't grab anything so down I go – plummeting out of sleep, drenched in perspiration.

Today's a good day; nothing to carry and no obstacles. I've even managed to find my way along the side of the ladder, by not looking down and keeping my eyes fixed on the gaudy cage. The going is easy now, and I can hear the bird screeching. I'm close enough to the cage to see the latch; less than a minute and I'll be there to open it. The bird is bouncing with anticipation, but now I'm here I don't know what to do, I'm scared.

Here she comes; today might be my lucky day, better get myself all spruced-up and ready to fly. Preen the gold feathers first, then the green, then the scarlet and finally the tiny azure ones around my eyes. I know she's wondering about what sort of bird I am. Isn't it obvious that I'm a phoenix? Bobbing up and down, waiting to be re-born in spectacular combustion.

This cage is made of gold, real gold not the sort that peels off after a few weeks. And the jewels, well they are fantastic! They set off my feathers a treat. Rubies, emeralds, carnelians, diamonds, sapphires, you name it I've got it. I know how to look good in my glitzy home but out there is where I need to be. I want to fly over towns, soar over mountains, even just perch in a tree. When you're free you can do what you want, go where any old whim takes you.

All I can do now is hop up and down and flap my wings in this gaudy prison. I don't know how long I've been in here; since she had the accident I suppose. Sliding down a steep hill on narrow pieces of wood strapped to her feet and supported by two sticks. Sounds daft to me. No wonder it all ended so badly.

Yes, there she is starting to walk up the steep bit. She can only do it when she's asleep, walk that is. When she's awake she has to lie flat. It's only when she dozes off that she starts to walk across the bridge; how far she gets depends on the medication she's had and how she's feeling that day. My only hope for freedom is that one day she makes it to the other side and lets me out.

Do you know, I've watched her plodding up that incline pushing a pram, other times a wheelchair and occasionally a shopping trolley. Once she was struggling with a wheelbarrow piled high with what looked like potatoes. As she tried to shove the load uphill the potatoes rolled off, so she stopped and picked them up. When she comes all loaded up with rubbish like that it's bloomin' obvious that she won't get across and let me out.

So it might be a long wait. As well as being steep, this bridge is poorly maintained. There's one bit on the downhill stretch where the stonework is so badly crumbled that they've had to put a ladder across the dilapidated bit. She's got that far a few times then fallen straight through the rungs, tumbling down to the river below.

I've tried to help her, believe me I have. "Mind the ladder! Mind the ladder!" I've shouted to her, but she either can't hear or doesn't understand me. The result is the same; she blunders onto the ladder and then goes head over heels, round and round, down and down and out of sight to me.

Another problem is that she's easily distracted. I've seen her get to the top and stop to admire the view, staying there gazing into the distance for so long that she's ready to wake up when she's only half way over the bridge. I've tried to tell her. "Keep going! Keep going! This is only a dream to you but it's real to me."

The bird is showing off its gorgeous plumage, tilting its head this way then that way so that the light catches on feathers of gold, scarlet and blue. Fabulous gemstones are glinting on the golden bars, shimmering with nuances of colour that don't occur in the real world. Or perhaps they do and I've just never seen them. I'm close enough now to be able to see the bird nibbling the catch with its beak, all the while looking directly at me, asking me to open the door and set it free. The door fastening is an elaborate mechanism crusted with diamonds around a huge carnelian. I rub my thumb over the deep red surface, willing my sleeping self and my waking self to believe the bird will be safe if I take the chance and let it go.

They pulled no punches at the hospital. If I have the operation I might be able to walk again. Or I might never walk again. I could die. It's a big risk: 50% chance of failure.

I can't believe it. She's got here at last. Now all she's got to do is open the door. I won't burst into flames right now; the operation comes first. She's worried something awful will happen to me. It won't. Everything'll be fine. Just open the door!

The bird is watching me, waiting for me, willing me to do it. I reach for the cage door. The bird waits.

About the author
Penny writes short stories, flash fiction and poetry. She is currently finishing a collection of short stories set in France during the early years of the twentieth century. During the late summer and autumn she makes all sorts of preserves using fruit and vegetables from her garden or foraged from the Dorset countryside. In the winter she knits and thinks of stories; some of these get written.

Perfect Justice

Paula R C Readman

I used to love my job, but not anymore. For fifteen years I enjoyed working for the building company Davidson Ltd. The wages were better than most. Then one morning everything changed. I don't like to use the word hate to describe how I felt on waking, but dread wasn't a strong enough word. Just the thought of having to deal with a certain person set my pulse racing.

Three years ago I always liked to arrive early for work to ensure everything was ready for Mr Davidson's arrival. *Efficiency* was his keyword. I always checked the emails for any new orders and restocked anything needed to complete jobs on time. Any problems or late orders I would print a copy of the details and place them on Mr Davidson's desk, along with a fresh cup of tea, so he had plenty of warning if anything might cause a delay.

"Timing is everything," Mr Davidson would say. "The earlier we know about problems, the quicker we can resolve them. Get your timing right and you can beat your competitors easily, while saving time and money, Brenda."

Then everything changed. I arrived at my usual time, after stopping off at a local newsagent to pick up a pint of milk, along with some fresh cakes for Mr Davidson's elevenses. The kettle had only just boiled, when to my surprise my boss buzzed. I hastily checked my watch. He was in early too. I made his tea and hurried through.

"Ah Brenda," he beamed.

I returned his smile. Anxious for the first time in all the years I had worked for him. I was about to ask if there was any problems, when he saved me the bother.

"Thank you for my tea. Please set it down there," he said, clearing a spot on his desk. "I have some good news."

I raised my notebook ready to start a dictation.

"No, no," he said. "The news doesn't really affect the rest of the staff. Today someone new is starting and I want you to show them the ropes. Please get them settled in as soon as possible, Brenda."

"Oh, yes, of course, Mr Davidson."

"Good." He reached for his phone and I took it as a sign of dismissal.

I lingered, unsure quite what he meant by *showing the ropes* to this unnamed person. When he showed no sign of acknowledging me, I gave a light cough.

"Yes, Brenda?" He held the phone from his ear; his finger paused over a button.

"Mr Davidson, hmm... what time will the person be arriving and what department am I to show them around?"

"Department? No, no, Brenda. She'll be working with you."

"Me!" I couldn't keep the shock out of my voice. Aghast that Mr Davidson felt the need to have someone else working with me.

I arrived back early from lunch and was shocked to discover a new desk in my office. It was much smaller than mine and it stood in a small dark alcove, facing a large free standing unit full of old company files.

I set my handbag down on my desk, as panic raced through my gut. *Where in hell was my computer?* Standing in its place was a new one. For a second I couldn't breathe and leant on the desk. All my work was gone, along with my belongings too. I let my breath out slowly. Shocked I reached for the phone and stabbed at the buttons.

"Aha, Brenda, you're back at last," Mr Davidson said.

Back at last! I hung the phone up. What in hell did he

mean? My lunch break had not finished. Unfazed by my look of annoyance he turned to speak to someone just out of my view. As my boss stepped aside a petite, bleached-blonde woman hesitated in the doorway. She smiled meekly up at him. Mr Davidson rested his hand on her back in a reassuring way. The woman didn't look like the type to need reassurance, not with her pencilled-in eyebrows and long red painted nails. Her attire of tight fitted white jeans, a skinny ribbed red jumper, and black stiletto heeled boots was more suited for an evening in a nightclub rather than for work.

"Brenda, this is Sabrina Perfect," my boss said, smiling broadly.

Ms Perfect lowered her head and smiled coquettishly at me, but my radar picked up trouble.

"She's here to help you." Mr Davidson pointed to the desk in the alcove. "Please move your belongings to that desk there."

To my surprise I realised that the tatty collection of dictionaries, *English Grammar,* and *Idiot's Guide To Computers* and spread sheet books were mine, so was the computer. Relief washed over me. I grinned through gritted teeth. "No need, sir. Someone has already done it."

"That's great. So, no time wasted, you can both get on with the job," he said to me, before turning to Sabrina. "Now, I hope you'll settle in quite quickly, Sabrina. If you need to know anything, please don't hesitate to ask Brenda."

Ms Perfect gave him a bright smile and then to my horror she winked at Mr Davidson, as he left the room.

From then on my serenity was shattered. No longer a shy little Miss, Sabrina became a chatterbox. Unsurprisingly her pet subject was herself. As for showing her the ropes I had to teach her the basics. She knew nothing, not even how to turn a computer on. Why did Mr Davidson feel I needed her here to run the office? Hadn't I been more than efficient?

By the end of the first day, all I really wanted to do was to show her how to hang herself. After the first week I was shattered and mentally drained. Once I used to be able to work at a leisurely pace. Now I seemed to spend most of my time playing catch-up with orders, while double-checking her work.

It wasn't just playing catch-up that took its toll on me, but having to endure her spiteful remarks.

"Brenda, when do you retire?"

"Retire? I'm not ready to retire yet."

"But you're old."

"Age is just a number."

"Well, when I get as old as you, I want to be doing something other than just this boring job."

I peered in her direction. She was watching again, waiting for a reaction to her comment. Whenever I caught her in the act, she wasn't a bit embarrassed and just smiled at me. My only relief came during lunchtime, or on overtime. Previously overtime wasn't something I had had to do, but it became a necessity much to my annoyance. One lunch break after Mr Davidson and Sabrina had left I settled down to work on a personal project. A knock at the door startled me. I hastily changed the screen and called, "Come in. It's unlocked,"

To my surprise Mrs Davidson entered. Tall and elegant she wore a figure-hugging dark brown tweed skirt suit and kitten-heeled black patent leather shoes that complemented not only her age, but her height and build. Her shoulder length light brown hair framed her perfectly made-up face. At first she looked quite youthful, but lines of concern around her eyes suggested to me that she was in her late forties, rather than her late thirties.

"Hello Brenda… Is my husband about?" she asked. I met her anxious face with a smile. "I'm sorry, but he's gone to lunch. Can I help?"

She hesitated for a second, before closing the door and gesturing to a chair, "May I?"

"Of course, Mrs Davidson, please do."

With poise she sat and crossed her fine ankles.

"I hope I'm not disturbing you, Brenda," she said, while glancing back at the door. "I was… hmm… well… you've worked with my husband for many years. I was wondering if…" She paused and bit her bottom lip as a heavy furrow marked her brow.

I smiled, hoping a look of patience showed on my face. That's when it dawned on me – she hadn't expected to find Mr Davidson here. She wanted to speak to me. Over the years I've worked for her husband I hadn't really had much contact with Mrs D. apart from an occasional brief phone call. "Hello, may I speak to my husband?" or in passing at the firm's Christmas do, "'Happy Christmas, Brenda." Therefore, I knew this was more than just a social chitchat.

She leant forward in a conspiratorial sort of way. "What I'm trying to say, Brenda, is you know my husband almost as well as I do. So I was wondering if you've seen any changes in his behaviour just lately."

"Changes, Mrs Davidson? I'm sorry I'm not sure what you mean?"

She glanced down, tugging at her wedding ring. "Brenda, how can I put this?" She didn't meet my eyes as she spoke slowly. "What I mean is, if it's possible, could you tell me if my husband and…?" A tiny sob broke free, as she lifted her tearful eyes to meet my puzzled expression.

The proverbial penny dropped. I realised just what her fear was. I nearly laughed in the poor woman's face. "Oh, Mrs Davidson, I can assure you that your husband isn't…"

I stuttered unable to complete the sentence. Personally I couldn't see Mr Davidson showing an interest in someone as shallow as Sabrina.

"Brenda, please call me Zara." A light flush coloured her cheeks as she handed me a small white business card. "All I'm asking is for you to let me know if he behaves out of character, that's all."

"I'm sorry Mrs Davidson... Zara, but..." I sought inspiration, not wanting to tell her I couldn't snoop on my boss. I studied her card for a moment and then dropped it on the corner of my desk. "Please, don't be offended, but I'm not sure if I'm the right person to ask. After all I only work for Mr Davidson."

She nodded, but I saw she wasn't satisfied.

Mrs D. studied her nails for a moment. Unlike Sabrina's long red ones, hers were short, squared, but well-manicured; a sign that she enjoyed gardening or doing housework.

"Brenda, I'm just a little concerned about my husband."

I stared at my computer wanting to get on with what I was doing before she'd interrupted. "Oh. Maybe he's anxious about the business, or something I'm not aware of?" I said.

Her face tightened and then with a half-smile, she said, "You're in a better position than I am to know about such things. Look, can I be honest with you?"

I nodded.

"This new secretary of his... she's so young."

Ahh, so little Miss Perfect was at the heart of all of this. "Well, I wouldn't call twenty-five young."

She gave a curt nod. "Why does he need her? When he's always been happy with your work, Brenda?"

I smiled. "I'm guessing with the increase in the workload, Mr Davidson has planned ahead." I said, feeling I owed some sort of loyalty to him. "That's why I'm working through my lunch break."

"Oh," she said, looking towards Sabrina's empty desk. "So why isn't she here too?"

My annoyance began to bubble up. I wanted to be honest, but instead I fudged the truth. "Well, she's not quite up to speed on some of the more important elements of the business. Zara, I'm sure you've nothing to worry about with Mr Davidson."

"Does *she* work *in* his office?"

"No," I said. "He buzzes me, if he wants something."

"Where are they both now?"

"Out to lunch," I said, pushing my spectacles up my nose, wishing only to get on with what I was doing.

"Together?"

"Zara, in all honesty, I cannot answer that, but I would say no. Sabrina left here alone. As you know Mr Davidson has his own private entrance into his office. I don't always know what time he leaves for lunch. Sometimes he'll call through to let me know if he's going onto another site straight afterwards. Today he didn't, so I'm sure he'll be back here by one, if you would like to wait in his office."

"No, no, that's quite all right," she said, heading for the door. "I'll see him at home." She paused briefly in the doorway. "Brenda, please contact me if you think there's something I should know about."

"Of course, Zara, I will."

Once she left, I briefly studied her business card again. The details were inscribed in gold calligraphy. I tore it up, dropping it in the waste basket and returned to my editing.

By the time Sabrina swanned in, lunchtime was well and truly over, but her lateness didn't bother me. I felt too smug to care.

"Good afternoon, Sabrina." I clicked send on an email

116

to myself. She leant against the shelving next to my desk, looking smug too.

I smiled at her, but she remained tight-lipped.

"Is everything all right, Sabrina?"

She looked me up and down. "You could do so much more with yourself, Brenda. You dress like an old biddy. What's this thing you have with cardigans, woollen skirts and granny shoes? Those round metal-rimmed glasses of yours are so passé.

"Passé?" I gave a light laugh. Shocked she knew the meaning of such a word.

"Sabrina, some of us are happy with the way we are." I opened a fresh document on my screen and hoped by ignoring her; she would go back to her own desk.

Out of the corner of my eye, I saw her staring at the floor. Then she bent, picked something up and studied it briefly, before continuing, "Maybe if you focused more on your appearance, you'd have better luck in finding a bloke."

"A bloke?" I let my breath out slowly to control my temper.

"Yes, every woman needs a bloke in their life. My mum says that's what makes a woman feel completely happy."

"Every woman!" I snapped, not wishing to hear anymore of her mother's wisdom.

"Yes. Nothing's going to stand in my way to be with my fellow," she stated, in a dark tone.

"I'm sure your mother is a wise lady, but you needn't concern yourself about me. Now we must concentrate on our work, so things get done a bit quicker around here."

Her bright red lips grinned back at me. She lowered her eyes, as though she was about to say something more, but I was focusing on my screen. Out of the corner of my eye, I saw her snatch something from the floor before returning to her desk.

117

For a while the office fell silent. I concentrated on checking the details for the company's next big project. When I say we worked in silence, I meant apart from the incessant clicking of Sabrina's plastic nails against her keyboard. I wanted so much to rip them off her fingers with pliers.

When I looked up again I was relieved to find it was nearly the afternoon tea break. I bent to pick my bag off the floor when a flash of white caught my attention. It was part of Mrs Davidson's business card. I popped it into the waste bin. I sensed Sabrina's eyes on me and knew she had more to say.

"Brenda, you're so last week's news. No decent guy would be interested in you."

"And you're not?" I knew as soon as the words were out of my mouth I shouldn't have reacted.

Sabrina giggled. "My mum said she knew the moment I was born that I was special. Perfect, in name and nature, is what she told everyone. She said that one day my face will grace the cover of every magazine and newspaper across the country, maybe even the world."

A pain crept up to my temple, as I clenched my teeth at her mother's wisdom.

She went on. "So Brenda what exactly have you got going for you? I mean unmarried at your age. Men must find you so dull and boring."

That was my fatal mistake. I allowed her to goad me into telling her my most passionate secret. I poured my heart out. Like the bittersweet taste of syrup the truth dawned on me. I should've known better. The glint in her eyes wasn't admiration, or even fascination, but her acknowledgement of finding my weak spot. Now she had ammunition to use against me. That's when I started planning my first crime novel, *Death of Little Miss Perfect*.

118

Over the next few months I planned how to commit the perfect murder. Every free second during the day I added notes to a file I kept on my computer. Then just before home time I would email a copy to myself. In the evening, I worked on the chapters, editing as I went along.

Sabrina became my muse. Every emotion of hatred that surfaced in me during the day, I poured into my creativity, allowing the words to flow from me. One day, while there was a lull in my work, I became so engrossed in adding ideas to my file I didn't notice Sabrina come up behind me, until her reflection appeared on my screen. Luckily, I flicked onto another screen, before she could read it.

"You know, you aren't supposed to do your own writing in work's time," she said in her mocking little girl tone.

I glared at her. "Haven't you got any work to do?"

"Plenty. Unlike you, it seems."

I opened the company emails hoping she would stop harassing me, but she was nowhere near finished.

"Isn't it about time you took a reality check, Brenda? You aren't ever going to be famous. You're such a loser." She adjusted her brightly coloured butterfly hair-clips before snatching up a folder. At the door, she flicked her bleached blonde hair over her shoulders, and grinned at me as she left the office.

The next morning before I had chance to boil the kettle, my boss summoned me to his office.

"Brenda, please come through right now..." he drew out the last word.

"I've just switched on the kettle, Mr Davidson."

"Forget about my tea."

"But I—" The phone went dead in my hand and cut off my sentence.

On entering his office he gestured impatiently to me

119

from behind his desk without looking up. "Shut the door, Brenda. Sit down."

My stomach sunk. It wasn't like him to ask me to sit. Without even making eye contact with me he went straight into what he had to say.

"It's been brought to my attention that on several occasions you've not been concentrating on your work."

I went to protest, but he silenced me with a flick of his hand.

"Up until now we've always been satisfied with your work, but just lately some important papers have gone astray."

"What papers? What are you saying?"

He glared at me. "I've been told that you're working on some book, Miss Wild—"

"But Mr Davidson it's only in my own time and break times."

"Well, I need you to concentrate more on the work you're paid for, not some future little dream of yours. Now, I'm sure you've plenty to do. And, if it's brought to my attention again, I shall have to take matters further."

I sat at my desk, fuming and re-evaluated my life. Mr Davidson had never criticised me before. I've always felt we had a great working relationship. We never engaged in personal chitchat, but there was a mutual understanding of each other. Hurt by his sudden change of attitude towards me, I began to think about all the new possibilities that could soon be opening up for me. I decided that anything was better than being stuck in an office staring at a shelf full of faded yellow files listening to Sabrina.

I clicked send on an email and muttered aloud, "Timing is everything."

The door burst open and Sabrina floated in, late as usual, humming to herself. She dumped her bag on her desk.

"Oh, good morning Brenda." Her self-satisfied smile dropped from her red lips at the sight of me. She perched on the edge of my old desk showing no sign of starting work. She briefly stared at her nails and began to chip away at the red varnish.

I wondered if Sabrina thought that I should dress in her style, with a peek-a-boo knickers skirt and ankle-breaking boots that screamed, *"Look at me! Look at me! Don't you think I'm sexy?"*

*"**Timing**,"* I muttered, focusing on my work while praying for the strength not to strangle her.

"Brenda?"

I pressed my lips into a pinched smile. "Yes?"

"I'm sorry, but yesterday when Mr Davidson asked me if I knew where some important documents were, I told him I didn't know."

Sabrina didn't seem to notice the anger settle on my face.

"Well, how was I to know that some silly designs for a house were that important?"

"Sabrina, all files are important. Please don't tell me they were the ones with the designer's notes about building changes on them?"

"I didn't think it mattered. I knew you would be able to produce another copy after I spilt my drink on them." She sighed gave a shrug and grinned at me as chips of red varnish fluttered to the floor like blood droplets.

Dear God, I thought, *please let me put her down now.*

She waffled on, while I tried to concentrate on what she was saying, but a beautiful image of her floated into my mind. She knelt before me, begging for my forgiveness, but I was enjoying the moment too much, as I fed her fingers into the paper shredder. Suddenly the delightful vision faded as her words penetrated.

121

"Of course, I wouldn't let myself go like some women," she giggled girlishly. "My mum says if you want to keep your man happy you need to look after your figure, especially when you reach a certain age, Brenda."

When I didn't answer her she sat down and began to work. The image in my head reformed itself. Sabrina seated in an electric chair, wearing a metal cap and shaking as I threw the switch. I imagined her brain frying. If she had one.

Once she focused on her work, I flicked back to my original screen and carried on editing my *Disposal of the Body* chapter.

"Brenda," she drew my name out in her childish annoying voice. "Have you ever thought about Botox?

"No, I haven't."

"If I was you, I would. You could lose those frown lines."

"Is that what you use then?" I kept my eyes on my screen.

"Please… tell me you're joking? I'm far too young to use Botox, but you aren't. You could get rid of those wrinkles and—"

I was no longer listening. That's it! Rat poison. Yes, of course. Why hadn't I thought of it? I looked up to find Sabrina watching me. I smiled while trying to picture her with a gag in her mouth buried alive somewhere.

As my novel came to its completion so Sabrina's life changed forever. In her normal cryptic way she chatted to me about it, but for some reason I was unable to blank her out as I had learnt to do in the past. She smugly informed me that her mother had been right.

"Sorry, your mother was right about what?" I met her stare.

"I knew you weren't listening to me," she said in her monotone voice. "I was saying you can get away with anything if you have a winning smile."

"And you do." I said without realising that for once it sounded like I was agreeing with her.

"Thank you, Brenda. Anyway, that's how I won my Mr Right. He told me it was the first thing he noticed about me. I'm so lucky to have been born with perfect teeth." She beamed at me with a smile that had as much appeal as a mouse from a cat.

I glanced over the top of my spectacles, but in my mind all I could picture was Sabrina's corpse, laid out in a coffin, with that same painted-on smile. With a nod, I said, "It's delightful."

The morning started as it usually did with Sabrina arriving late. However, on this particular Monday morning, while the kettle was boiling, I checked my private email account and discovered an email from a publisher.

"Timing is everything." I left Mr Davidson's tea to stew, not caring about it for once. I printed off the email and began the process of deleting all my personal files from the company computer.

"Morning Brenda." Sabrina finally arrived and plonked herself down on the corner of her desk. "Has Martin spoken to you yet?"

"Don't you mean Mr Davidson?" I watched the final folder deleting and then emptied the recycle bin and history folder, before meeting her eyes.

She cocked her head on one side and smirked at me just as Mr Davidson opened his office door and called, "Brenda, please come here for a moment. Don't worry about my drink."

I slipped the email into my cardigan pocket as I entered his office.

"Please sit down." He gestured to a chair, as he perched on the front of his desk.

I noticed he looked different. Gone was his dark business suit and formal tie. Now he wore a casual jacket and trousers. Over the weekend his hair had changed colour too. His temples no longer showed signs of grey.

"I'm sorry to have to inform you, but the company needs to make some cutbacks, and with a heavy heart Brenda—"

Before he had chance to finish his speech, I stood and smiled at him. Without another word, he handed me a letter.

"Please don't worry about working up to the end of the month. You'll find a bit extra in your pay-packet. Once you've cleared your desk, you can go."

For a moment I pondered about telling him my news, but he had already returned to his seat. As he sat staring at his computer screen I knew it was pointless to expect him to thank me for my loyalty and hard work.

On closing the office door for the last time, I grasped the email in my pocket and grinned to myself.

At my desk I found Sabrina busy packing my things into a box. She looked up with a creamy cat-like smirk.

"Dear Brenda, now, don't you go upsetting yourself." She emptied the contents of my drawer into the box. "There's no point in crying over spilt milk, as my mum is fond of saying. Though, in all honesty, you did bring it upon yourself."

"I did what?"

"You told Martin's wife about us."

"I've no idea what you're talking about, Sabrina."

"Oh yes, you did. I found part of her business card by your desk. You should have kept your nose out of other people's business. My mum says—"

I ignored her, picked up my bag and headed for the door.

"What about your things?" she snapped.

"You keep them, you'll need them..." I allowed the door to slam shut.

So many unbelievable things have happened in the time since I've left the company. With the first print run of my book I've been busy promoting and doing signings around the country, so I hadn't really noticed how much time had passed.

In my excitement at seeing my name on the cover of my novel, I sent a signed copy to my old boss as a thank you for introducing me to Sabrina. Bitchy, I know, but hey, he did me a favour, didn't he?

While working on my second novel I rented a holiday cottage in Cornwall, a sort of self-imprisonment. One morning I decided to take a well-earned break from the writing and headed to the local shop for supplies. As I passed the newsagent window I saw Sabrina's smiling countenance staring back at me.

On entering the shop I found most of the newspapers carried the same beaming photograph of her on all their covers. However, what intrigued me most was one of the headlines, *Best-selling Novel Leads to Cold Blooded Murder.*

I purchased a copy and sat on the seawall to read it. The paper stated:

Yesterday a police spokesperson confirmed that the body of a woman found in the Sussex holiday home of the businessman, Martin Davidson, was that of his missing secretary, Miss Sabrina Perfect.

Perfect's family had reported her missing two months earlier after she failed to return home from a holiday she had taken abroad. The paper went on to report that the police had arrested and charged Zara, the wife of Martin Davidson for the unlawful killing of Miss Perfect.

Another bizarre twist to the case has since come to light that might explain what led up to the death of Ms Perfect. A novel found at the crime scene, titled *The Perfect Murder* had been written by the former secretary of Martin Davidson, Miss Brenda Wild.

When the story broke our reporter was unable to track down the author for her reaction, but her publisher has stated that her book is now on its fourth reprint.

I lowered the newspaper, and stared out across the harbour. The gulls sailed on the light breeze. I mulled over whether sending Zara a copy of my book was a bad idea, as she may have misinterpreted my reason for sending it. Did she think it was a sign to tell her that her husband was up to no good with his new secretary?

I tucked the newspaper under my arm and headed back to the cottage knowing my publisher would be very interested in my second novel. I laughed to myself which startled a fisherman on the harbour. At least Sabrina's Mum was right about one thing, I thought, while unlocking the cottage door; Little Miss Perfect did make the front pages after all.

About the author

Since 2010 Paula has been published by English Heritage, Bridge House Publishing, Springbok Publications, Parthian Books, Black Hare Press, Blood Song Books, Kandisha Press and Chapeltown Books. In 2012, she was the overall winner of World Book Day short story competition run by Austin Macauley publishers, and Writing Magazine/ Harrogate Crime Writing Festival short story competition, too. In February 2020, she had her first crime novella *The Funeral Birds* published by Demain Publishing. In June Bridge House Publishing published thirteen dark tales by Paula in *Days Pass Like a Shadow*. In August Paula's first crime novel *Stone Angels* was published by Darkstroke.

Blog: https://paularcreadmanauthor.blog

Shadow Dancers

Cathy Leonard

She loved trees in winter. The gnarled blackened barks split down the middle. Siamese twins warring with each other. She saw dancers, warriors, tai-chi masters – gathering the stars, bowing to the moon. Shadow boxers. Shadow puppets.

She photographed these, dozens of them, and hung them in her hallway, its walls painted in coconut twist, a pale cream with a tinge of pink, a canvas for her shadow dancers. Then Michael asked her to give up her coconut twist bungalow and move into his spacious flat overlooking the bay.

"It doesn't make sense. You're always here anyway!" he argued.

"That's not true."

"Mostly true?

"Sometimes true."

She liked his huge bay window that poured sea light on his bed every morning. She liked his high corniced ceiling, his cast iron fireplace with the Victorian tile inset. She liked his steel sprung sofas and marble topped tables with carved mahogany legs, his stone hot water bottle and his silver hand grinder. She revelled in the wine-reds and night-sky blues of his Kashmir rugs and the smell of dust that clung to his heavy window drapes. But most of all she loved his frayed wallpaper where cupids and shepherdesses disported themselves recklessly on some Elysian plain.

Her shadow dancers could not compete with these Grecian foibles. They needed a blank space on which to sketch their stark poses. She wondered how long Michael would allow this glorious revelry to continue; he didn't seem to notice their state of disrepair and disarray. And that was the problem. Michael didn't seem to notice anything.

He would happily hang her Shadow Dancers on these walls and not see how ugly their choreographed limbs would look set against the pastoral anarchy that reigned here; Michael did not notice such things.

He did not know when her stillness needed to be stirred. He caught none of her shifts in mood and she could find none in him. She found his will to complacency a lump of unleavened dough between her fingers, and knead as she would, she was unable to make it yield to her touch. There was no yeast in it. So she decided to cover the dough and leave it and hope that it might prove.

And still he asked her to give up her coconut twist walls, and still she could not explain, and then it happened.

She returned home one day to find a gin bottle in the middle of the floor and the DVD player pulled out of its niche, her wardrobe ransacked, and her favourite coat, a shabby Avoca tweed, her beloved Canon camera and her Shadow Dancers gone. In disbelief she scoured the hedges, gardens and laneways in search of them.

"They must have been disturbed," said Sergeant Doyle. "They usually take the electricals. A tweed coat? That'll be to wrap up the booty. And were the pictures valuable?"

Valuable? Margaret thought about the word. Latin in origin? Valuare, valuatum. She couldn't remember.

"No. Yes. I mean yes… to me."

"Are you sure they didn't take cheques from your cheque book. They remove them from the back so that you won't notice."

"No. They're all there."

"And the camera?"

"I liked it a lot. It takes time to get to know a camera. Like a relationship." On seeing his blank expression she added, "It was a Canon. I'd have to look up the model number."

"And its value?"

"I've had it a while."

"The insurance company will need a statement with figures and model numbers. You wouldn't think of getting an alarm system?"

Alarm bells punctuating the night silence, disturbed by a breeze or a wrong sequence entered after a late night out. No she wouldn't consider it.

She wrote poems about the burglary and read them to her creative writing group. The words "looted", "plundered" and "violated" figured a lot. Someone asked her if she'd been raped. Margaret was stunned into a silence that could not be stirred.

She sat on her haunches in corners of the house and never went out. She took sick leave from work. She dreamt of a house with no doors, an open skied cylinder leaking rain on its heirlooms. She woke up sobbing, her whole body aching with the pain of something that felt like loss. She developed a chest infection that would not clear.

Michael bought her a new camera which she wrapped in a woollen jumper and stowed under the bed for safe keeping. She lay inert, unresponsive and silent as he watched her at night. She would waken, choking on her dreams. Silent tears streaked her hair grey overnight.

She threw away her bohemian attire, her scalloped edged jumpers, her sequined cottons reeking of sandalwood. She wore polo neck acrylics and polyester trousers in shades of grey and brown. Michael gave up his sunlit-frayed shepherdesses and moved into the coconut twist bungalow in suburbia. Margaret went back to work.

She stood in front of a group of Year 8s, every muscle in her body taut, her teeth clenched, trying to hold their concentration in this jug that was the class room; knowing that at any moment the jug would spill over or even crack.

"Miss, can somebody open a window, I'm roastin'!"

"But it's freezin' Miss!"

"There's a wasp in your hair, Sarah Casey!"

"Oh Miss!"

And she watched the liquid rise in the jug and dribble all over the floor.

She was aware of the profile of the Deputy Principal in the glass panel on her left, always patrolling the corridor for just such leaks. The thought of shadow dancers flitted and vanished.

"Now that's enough girls," she said, too quietly.

If she was lucky the bell would ring. Books would shut, catapult into desks. Lids would slam, desks scrape and a flurry of girls would squeeze themselves through the doorway and expand into the corridor.

The Principal was glad to get rid of her.

Michael now did all the cooking and cleaning and washing. He weeded the garden and planted spring bulbs. All winter the new camera lay in its nest of wool beneath the bed and still Margaret mourned. She watched triangles of light brighten the neighbour's gable wall. She watched the dying fuchsia boxing with the wind and thought to write a poem. She watched Michael come and go. It was like the time she had broken her arm and was untouchable. They watched each other now through this barrier of a broken arm's length and waited.

A kitten circling the tall stalks of spring daffodils caught her unawares. It may have been his shade of tortoise shell or the pose in with which he gathered himself for pounce. She reached for the camera, fumbled with the unfamiliar dials, her mind dazed with the possibilities. She pressed a button and the thing sprang into action.

131

"There's a handbook to go with it," he said from the doorway. And looking at his face a knowing stirred in her.

She knew that the dough had been left to prove for long enough and she stretched out her arm towards him.

About the author

Cathy has been writing and teaching for over thirty years. She has published poetry, short stories and children's stories and has been shortlisted for a number of awards, runner up in the Fish Flash Fiction Award 2013 and the Sceine Poetry Competition 2014. She had a short story selected for publication in *Baubles* 2016 and *Glit-er-ary* 2017. Cathy lives in Dublin with her husband Stephen, Molly, her trusty red-setter cross and new arrival– a stray one eyed three month old kitty – Sherlock. Now all she needs is a Watson!

https://bake-a-yarn.blogspot.com/

Taming Fate

Dawn Knox

A bullet through the brain would be quick.

But Robert knew how messy that would be because he'd seen the result twice during his time in the trenches of northern France. Fellow officers who'd reached the limit of their endurance and had chosen to end it all.

And Mama loathed untidiness.

Nevertheless, it was Robert's Option One.

His pistol was hidden in the drawer and the deed could be done without much effort.

He wasn't afraid of pulling the trigger neither did he fear he'd break Mama's heart.

He wasn't sure she had one.

There was none of that feeble, feminine nonsense about his mother.

And perhaps it had served her well because she'd been able to carry on when her husband had died in Flanders and her son had returned from the Somme in a wheelchair.

Robert knew the townsfolk considered Mama tough and intimidating. There was no need to waste their sympathy on the widow of brave Colonel Reginald Murray and mother of poor, crippled Captain Robert Murray. Her emotional strength served her well in in a post-war town; running the mansion, the estate and various charitable committees while her son frittered away his time in a wheelchair either in the garden or staring out of a window.

Robert knew he was incidental to the running of the household. Things carried on around him. Things were done *to* him and *for* him.

He was irrelevant.

When the weather was pleasant, he was wheeled into

the garden in the shade of the trees, and now, as he sat on the lawn and stared at the gleaming lake in the distance, Robert considered Option Two. He wondered how long it would take for anyone to miss him should he quietly wheel himself down to the water's edge… and keep going.

Drowning would take more effort but be cleaner than blowing out his brains and far easier for his mother to explain. He imagined her saying, "There's a slope leading down to the lake, you see. Poor Robert obviously hadn't been able to stop the wheelchair and it rolled into the water. With his legs being paralyzed, he wouldn't have stood a chance… Such a tragedy. He was a kind, young man, with so much to offer."

The rattle of cup against saucer brought Robert back to the present. The young girl, who he recognised as Cook's granddaughter, was limping towards him across the lawn, carrying his tea. Her face was set rigid with the effort of keeping the tray level as she lurched from side to side, one leg clamped tightly in a brace. Robert had occasionally noticed the girl around the house. And indeed, recently, he'd seen her more frequently.

Now, however, he held his breath. For some reason, it was important to him that she reached the table without falling over or dropping anything. Perhaps because her face displayed such fierce determination which betrayed how crucial it was to *her*.

Finally, she reached him and placing the tea things on the table in front of him, she allowed herself a glimmer of a triumphant smile.

"Alice! Alice!" Cook's voice, sharp and agitated, could be heard some way off.

"Gran didn't think I could do it," the girl said, "but I can do more than peel spuds and shell peas."

She seemed to be speaking more to herself than to him.

Then turning, she stumbled slightly, righted herself and set off back towards the kitchen.

"Wait!" called Robert. "Alice, is it?"

He had no idea why he wanted to detain her. Perhaps he needed a distraction. Mulling over the options for ending his life was draining.

Depressing, even.

"Yes, sir. Alice. That's me," she called over her shoulder but before he could reply, Cook appeared, her cheeks redder than usual and one hand on her cap to keep it in place as she lumbered across the grass towards her granddaughter. She stopped, her eyes darting from Robert to Alice and back again, attempting to determine how much of an annoyance the girl might have been and how the young master was responding.

"Alice?" Cook said nervously. "Come along now! I told you not to touch that tray! You shouldn't be bothering Captain Murray."

She hadn't said 'Poor Captain Murray' but her tone had certainly suggested it.

"Ah, Mrs Connor," said Robert. "Alice has been no trouble and I was about to ask her to pour my tea. I trust I'm not keeping her from the kitchen..."

"Uh, no, sir. That's all right with me." She turned to Alice. "You come back to the kitchen immediately you've finished, do you understand, my girl?" she said in a loud whisper.

"I'm not supposed to be here," Alice said matter-of-factly when her grandmother had gone. "Your Ma don't like it. She says I should be in school."

Alice tucked a wisp of straggly hair behind her ear and poured tea into a cup.

"So, why aren't you?" he asked.

She snorted with derision. "I don't like school."

135

"Nobody *likes* school. It's just something children have to do." He thought back to his schooldays. Harsh, unforgiving and often painful. Papa had paid handsomely for the privilege of sending his son to the same school that he'd attended, and Robert suspected they'd both been equally unhappy there.

"The others laugh and stare at my leg. And they go off an' play. I have to sit there watching. I'd rather be here helping Gran," she said.

"How old are you, Alice?"

"Ten." She bit her bottom lip and stared at her feet.

Robert guessed her real age was eight or nine. She was so small. Delicate, like a baby bird partially caged in the leg brace.

"Can you read?" he asked.

"Yes." Her gaze alighted on the newspaper on the table between the tray and chess board. "Well, I can read simple words," she added, as if she feared he might test her.

"Can you write?"

She nodded. "Can't see the point though. Reading and writing don't help me wash up."

"There's more to life than washing up," he said. "One day when you're older, you might want to do something different. Now the war's over, women are being employed in all sorts of jobs."

She shrugged. "Ain't no one going to want to employ me." She looked down at her leg.

"But if you can read and write, they might. Life's full of interesting opportunities if you look for them."

She put her head on one side as if considering his words.

"Can *you* read and write?" she asked.

"Of course."

"Why ain't you doing something more interesting then?"

For an instant, he wondered how to respond. By rights, he should be outraged at her impertinence but instead, he felt amused. How strange that this straggly-haired child had been brave enough to voice her opinion. So far, even his mother had tiptoed around him, only hinting at the thoughts which he knew to be on her mind.

At Robert's smile, Alice's hands locked into fists and she held her arms rigidly at her sides. "You're laughing at me," she said crossly. "I thought *you'd* understand."

"I do," said Robert quickly.

"P'raps It's all right for people who've got lots of money, to learn to read and write and then spend all day staring into the distance like you do."

"Possibly," he conceded.

"Well, some of us 'ave got work that needs to be done," she said and turned on her heel.

"Wait! Alice!"

She stopped and looked back at him.

He didn't want her to go. She was impudent but full of life.

"Would you like a slice of cake?" He indicated the plate on the tray.

"I already took a bit," she said with an impish grin, and limped away.

That night after Robert had been put to bed, he slipped the pistol out of his bedside table and ran his finger along the cold, smooth barrel. For some reason, it made him think of the metal rods which were strapped to either side of Alice's leg – unyielding and constraining.

Load it.

Aim.

Squeeze the trigger.

His pointless life would be over. One less problem for everyone.

137

He allowed his mind to explore the possibility but instead of the welcoming blackness he'd conjured up when he'd considered ending it all before, now all his mind's eye could see was the frail, skinny figure of Alice – her unsteady gait hampering her progress as she determinedly made her way across the dappled lawn and back to her life of drudgery.

He doubted she'd given him another thought. After all, she hadn't served his tea on the lawn because she'd cared about his needs – it had simply been a challenge. His death would mean nothing to her. And yet, having watched her resolve as she tottered across the grass, he'd been touched and he couldn't get the image out of his mind. Like a frail bird which needed protecting. So much determination and purpose gleamed in her eyes. He envied her that. And yet, in avoiding school, she was hiding away from real life, just like him.

I thought you'd understand, she'd said crossly as if assuming they were kindred spirits with a special bond between them because of their disabilities. But what did *she* know? She was simply a child. How could this urchin possibly understand the things he'd seen, the things he'd done, the things he'd failed to do…? She had no idea of the blackness in his soul.

He sighed and placing the pistol back in the drawer, he switched out the light.

Morning arrived grey and brooding. Leaden clouds moved briskly across the sky, driven by a cold breeze and by the time Robert was dressed and ready to face the day, rain was lashing the gardens and the wind was agitating the surface of the lake. Today was not a day for sitting on the lawn.

After breakfast, a maid reported to his mother that water was dripping from the ceiling in one of the bedrooms and once again, Robert's feelings of inadequacy were reinforced. He could neither temporarily mend the roof, nor engage someone to do a lasting repair. Of course, he was perfectly capable of using the telephone and contacting a workman – but there was no need, his mother informed him. She would deal with it.

He wheeled his way to the library. Not because he wanted to read but because it was one of the few rooms his mother avoided. It had been his father's refuge.

"That room is too gloomy," his mother had declared and Robert fought hard to ensure she didn't carry out her threat to redecorate. He liked to close his eyes and breathe in the odours that reminded him of his father: the pipe smoke which persistently clung to the velvet curtains, the smell of the leather-bound books and the beeswax polish on antique wood. Each day, Robert fancied the aromas faded slightly and he dreaded the thought of them vanishing altogether. It was almost worth remaining alive to defend the library from his mother's attempts to freshen it up. It gave him a purpose. It felt strangely fulfilling to have a goal, however trivial and pitiful it might be.

Annoyance washed through him as the library door opened.

The maid looking for more leaks? Or worse, his mother?

But it was neither. Instead, the diminutive figure of Alice stood frozen in shock. Her usual impertinence had deserted her and her mouth opened and closed as she tried to think of an explanation for her presence in the library. He knew there was no reason for her being there. Cook certainly wouldn't have sent her. But perhaps like him, she'd sought solitude.

"No potatoes to peel today?" he asked and he smiled to show she wasn't in trouble.

"Done 'em," she said with a defiant toss of her head, then added a polite "sir." presumably in recognition that this was no time for insolence. Meanwhile her hands fumbled behind her back, seeking the door handle in order to escape.

"Were you looking for something?" he asked softly, his smile, open and welcoming, his tone gentle.

She hesitated but when he smiled and appeared to be waiting for a reply, she said shyly, "I just wanted to look at that..." She pointed at the large world globe, "and the books."

"Did you want any particular book?"

"No." She frowned as if the thought that she might want to look in one book rather than another, hadn't occurred to her.

"I just like to see them all lined up on the shelves," she said.

He wanted to smile at the thought of anyone admiring books for their appearance and arrangement, rather than their content.

"Is there something you wanted to see on the globe?" he asked, following her line of gaze.

"No. I just wondered if it spins like the one at school. Mrs Parsons always chooses her favourites to spin it. She don't ever pick me."

"Well, come and spin this one," he said.

"Oh! Can I?"

Her eagerness touched him. "Of course!"

She limped towards the desk and placing a tentative finger on the middle of Africa, she swiped gently and set it in motion.

"Do you know where England is?" he asked as they watched the earth spinning on its axis.

She frowned and shrugged.

140

Robert stopped the globe and pointed at the British Isles.

"It's very small," she observed. "What's that one?" She indicated a large area.

"That's the United States of America."

"How d'you know? You're too far away to read the writing."

"I recognise the shape and position."

Her eyes widened as if she were impressed.

"Can you recognise Passchendaele?" she asked, squinting at the names on the surface of the globe.

"It's here," he said and she gently placed her finger on the spot he'd indicated.

"That's very small," she said doubtfully. "Are you sure?"

He nodded and sighed.

"My brother, Frank's buried there," she whispered.

Robert's heart lurched. Another young man lost in the muddy, bloody trenches of Flanders.

"One day," she said wistfully, "I'm going to go to…"

He'd anticipated she was about to say 'Passchendaele' or 'Flanders', so he was surprised when she added, "London."

"Frank always said he'd take me there and show me where the King lives. I'll have to go on me own now." She sighed.

As she clasped her hands together, her skinny elbows poked out sideways reminding Robert of a scrawny bird about to take flight. How wonderful it would be if she really could fly. What a happy release to know she could take to the skies and that her leg was no encumbrance at all. Then she could go anywhere in the world.

That night at dinner, his mother began to speak in what Robert recognised as her jocular voice. It was the way she

141

delivered a message she knew wouldn't be welcomed by the recipient.

"Guess who I bumped into at Dorothea Thomsett's this afternoon!"

She didn't wait for his response.

"Sir William Grosvenor! Fancy that! Yes!" she continued as if he'd expressed the surprise and delight she was displaying. "And you'll never guess what! Despite his incredibly heavy workload, he's offered to see you..." She paused and unable to meet his eyes, she picked up her wineglass and studied its contents.

Robert merely sighed. Sir William was the fourth eminent consultant his mother had contacted. The three previous doctors had prodded, poked and ordered tests but in the end, they'd agreed – the damage to Robert's spine was so great, he would never walk again. One of them had even expressed the opinion that Robert was lucky to be alive.

Would Sir William find anything different to the others?

Of course not. But it seemed his mother wasn't about to give up on her quest to restore the use of his legs.

"So...?" she asked uncertainly. "Shall I tell him we'll see him next Wednesday?"

He was aware she was holding her breath, waiting for him to agree to her plans. The last appointment she'd arranged had resulted in a huge row and he was surprised she was attempting to manipulate him again. But it seemed her desire to have an able-bodied son was overriding the risk of an argument.

Robert was weary. How many times did he have to tell her that no amount of money or wishful thinking was going to restore the feeling in his legs?

"Robert?" the falsely jovial tone was becoming strident.

If he refused, she'd shout and they would argue. Unless...

"I'll go, on one condition," he said so abruptly she almost dropped her glass.

"Condition? What on earth do you mean, Robert?" She wasn't used to her wishes being limited by terms.

"I'll go to the appointment next Wednesday, so long as Sir William also sees Alice and we pay for her consultation."

"Alice? Who on earth do you mean?"

"Mrs Connor's granddaughter."

"Robert! You're not seriously suggesting I should bother such an eminent doctor with the cook's granddaughter?"

Robert wondered if he'd done the right thing in insisting Mrs Connor and Alice accompany them in the chauffeur-driven car to London but it hadn't made sense for Benson to drive him and his mother to Harley Street and for Cook and her granddaughter to take the train.

Now, the five occupants of the car were travelling through the countryside in oppressive silence.

Mrs Murray clasped the handbag on her lap with gloved hands and with her head turned, she stared out of her window at the passing scenery, studiously ignoring Mrs Connor in the front passenger seat with a wriggling Alice on her lap.

The cook sat rigidly in her seat, as if to show she knew better than to assume an ease and familiarity she wasn't entitled to in the presence of her employer and periodically she softly reprimanded the fidgeting, chattering child.

Benson drove silently as usual although Robert could see his eyes in the rear-view mirror and knew he was glancing around the car, aware of the tension.

Alice, alone, seemed unperturbed by the conventions of

society and from time to time, she glanced at Robert over her grandmother's shoulder, smiling at him and nibbling her lower lip as if the pleasure couldn't quite overcome the nerves.

How refreshing it was to see the familiar journey through Alice's eyes and to delight in the sights he usually overlooked, especially once they reached London.

"This isn't the way to Harley Street, Benson," Mrs Murray said sharply as the chauffeur indicated to turn right.

Robert quickly explained he'd requested they pass Buckingham Palace before their appointments so Alice would be able to see the place her brother had promised to show her.

He noticed his mother's jaw clench. "I see. Well, let's hope we make it to Sir William's on time," she said in the clipped tones she'd used when she'd agreed to Robert's terms and when he'd insisted Alice took the first appointment.

What was the world coming to when servants took precedence over their betters? she'd asked crossly.

He'd pointed out that it didn't matter who Sir William saw first. A doctor should treat all patients equally. His mother had merely sniffed and had obviously decided to silently endure her son's unreasonable demands, so long as he agreed to see the physician.

It wouldn't make any difference whether Robert was early or late for his appointment. Mama would learn soon enough there was no hope his mobility would be restored.

Hope. What an interesting concept.

From his first day in the trenches in 1914, hope had deserted him. Well, deep down, he must have been optimistic that he and his men would win the day's battle and still be alive to see nightfall. But as the war dragged on, hope seemed futile. Everything was determined by Fate. It

144

didn't matter how much effort one put into an endeavour or how deserving one was. In the end, Fate decided.

And Fate was fickle.

No, not fickle, because that implied a randomness which had equal odds.

But that wasn't correct.

Fate, it seemed, was *vindictive*.

Many of those in Robert's company had died despite his struggle to ensure their safety and he himself, had survived four years of hardship only to be shot days before the Armistice. Now, for him, there was no hope of walking again, no hope of a fulfilling life and no hope for a meaningful future. The only control he had over his existence was the ability to end it at his time of choosing. And of course, the method he chose to finish it. Leaving things to Fate was simply asking for grief.

He glanced around Sir William's luxurious waiting room. His mother was pretending to read a magazine. She alternated between glancing at the elegant grandfather clock and inspecting her wrist watch.

She sighed.

She tutted.

She tapped her foot and drummed her fingers on the soft, velvet arm of her chair. Unlike his mother, Robert dreaded Alice's consultation finishing. While she was behind the mahogany, double doors with the doctor, anything was possible. Once they came out and the verdict was delivered, there would be no turning back. For good or ill, Alice's future would be decided.

To his surprise, Robert found he was *hoping* and was immediately angry with himself for once again being fooled into believing Fate might play fair.

He squeezed his eyes tightly shut and silently pleaded

with anyone or anything that might be listening to his thoughts.

Allow me a miracle. Please.

Not for a cure for himself.

Heal Alice, he begged silently. His plea was as much for Alice's leg as for his own peace of mind. Being able to walk without the brace would obviously improve her quality of life but for himself, he wanted proof that Fate was not malicious – that there could be rewards and not just unfailing punishment.

But suppose Fate denied Robert his miracle and the doctor could do nothing to help Alice?

Then I will fight it, he thought.

He gripped the arms of his wheelchair tightly. Whatever the outcome, Robert vowed to assume the role of benefactor to the young girl. No one would know, especially not Alice herself and above all, he would conceal it from his mother who wouldn't approve of him taking an interest in a servant's grandchild.

That skinny, insolent child had saved her son's life by giving him purpose – Mama would never suspect that. Robert would put aside all thoughts of suicide and instead, observe from afar to see how he could help the girl. How ironic that his mother would never know how close *she'd* come to losing her son and how *his* mind had been changed by the young girl.

The double mahogany doors opened and Robert and his mother sat upright. Mrs Murray keen to see her son being the focus of Sir William's attention. Robert holding his breath, waiting to see if Fate had heeded his plea. It was hard to tell the outcome of the consultation from Mrs Connor's expression. She dabbed her eyes as she shepherded the young girl from the doctor's office.

But Alice was grinning, her eyes glowing, and

immediately, Robert knew the news was good. Mrs Murray beamed proprietorially although Robert knew her delight was not for Alice but because it gave her hope that Sir William would also be able to help her son. Success bred success. The more illustrious Sir William's reputation and the more successful his results, then surely, the more likely he'd be to help her son.

Sir William remained cautious about Alice, not promising she would eventually walk normally but at least he seemed optimistic and had agreed to treat her. If he succeeded, her future could be remapped. She would have possibilities.

She would have more than that. If she wouldn't return to school, he'd tutor her himself. Secretly, he would settle a small amount of money on her – just enough for her to be comfortable.

Whatever the future, Robert vowed, he'd force Fate to relinquish the key to her bird cage and then he would open the door and set her free to fly away.

About the author

Dawn's latest books are *The Macaroon Chronicles* and *The Basilwade Chronicles*, both published by Chapeltown Books. She enjoys writing in different genres and has had romances, speculative fiction, sci-fi, humorous and women's fiction published in magazines, anthologies and books. Dawn has also had two plays about World War One performed internationally. You can follow her here on https://dawnknox.com.

The Holiday

Jeanne Davies

Humming came naturally as she sorted through the laundry from the washing-line. It encapsulated the precious aroma of fresh air and sunshine. Folding crisp white cotton, smoothing windblown creases, singing gently, always enlivened her senses. A smile played upon her lips as she allowed memories to ricochet around in her head. Years ago, her mother only had a copper which she toiled over as she boiled up all her whites, sheets, and towels, poking it with her long wooden pinchers. She remembered the sweat prickling across her mother's brow, picking up the light in a rainbow shape above her sparse pencilled-in eyebrows. Looking back now, Matilda likened her mother's concentration over the brew to that of a witch stirring her cauldron.

"Get your wellies on and come out to the mangle with me, Tilly," her mother would sigh, as she dragged the steaming laundry across from the copper to the clinical white china of the Belfast sink.

The mangle constantly filled Matilda with dread when she was a young girl. It was a cold sinister object that hid behind the shed. She always approached it with caution as something about it resembled a contraption used for torture during the Victorian era. She always seemed to be the one feeding the machine with the wet clothes whilst her mother's strong arm tirelessly cranked the ornate wrought iron wheel around rhythmically. Sometimes her tiny fingers would get too close to the stone rollers and a few times they unexpectedly got pinched; especially vulnerable was the long middle finger on her left hand. She always felt it was unfair that her two brothers were never asked to perform such a task. Although still damp, the folded sheets would come through the mangle looking as though they were already ironed, whereas bath towels usually needed a second run through as they were still wet. In the winter months, her hands would be blue with cold as she stood handing over pegs to her mother. Once the washing was on the line it was free to dance and play in the wind, sometimes tumbling over itself like a circus clown. She would watch the clothing wave at her from the line and imagine the psyches of the wearers still inhabiting those garments. On the way back down the garden path from picking gooseberries from her father's allotment, Matilda would swing around the prop, inhaling deeply the fresh smell of the laundry. She would take delight in imagining the sheets were curtains on a huge stage from where she would appear ready to perform a ballet dance in a tutu.

Humming finished; Matilda stood back to admire the victorious pile of laundry plumped high on the bed. The bed... so ancient and flaccid; too many reminiscences to recall, but here it still was. She stood there for a while combing through her thoughts. Once it held their lovers' passion, comforted babies, was strewn with wrapping paper as children opened their Christmas stockings and it eventually became a merciful place of rest and relief from pain. Now it was just a restless place engulfed in loneliness. There were no regrets. Fred and she had a real marriage, embracing the good times together and weathering the bad, holding each other close through every storm. Looking back now it seemed even the bad times were great. They'd had a wonderful life together... true love, so deep and painfully real, cut deeper than either of them could ever have known at the start. She still couldn't believe that he was gone. Despite being grateful that his suffering had ceased, she sometimes felt angry that he'd left her alone.

Many empty years had drifted by since the bewilderment of the funeral when her heart had been ripped open, never to be repaired. The coldness of the graveyard yesterday still brought tears.

Her mother's ancient aspidistra plant touched her like a vacant tongue as she made her way to the spare bedroom. She'd told Matilda that she'd saved the plant during the war by taking it down into the air-raid shelter with her. The bedroom door was stiff as it was rarely used these days but with a bit of force it creaked painfully open. She looked up through the myriad of tiny dust particles twinkling like shooting stars around the room and there it was on top of the big wardrobe, their ancient well-travelled luggage set. She heaved it on to the bed, the musky smell invading her nose immediately as she opened the smallest of the scruffy suitcases. It was like opening Pandora's box. A further shower of particles spiralled with a puff into the air like a genie from a bottle. Her fingers trembled as she touched the countless wounds imbedded in the pungent brown leather, trying to remember where each one had come about. She felt the memories gather and gently ripple through her mind, the places they'd visited, amazing times in remarkable places. On their last holiday to South America she'd made him wear green gaucho pants and a sombrero hat. Fred didn't mind; nothing fazed him.

Matilda had spent a long time mulling things over before she had agreed to take this latest trip. Melancholy suddenly swept in a dark cloak around her shoulders which forced her to leave the room. She grasped on to the kettle handle to steady herself, appreciating its reassuring warmth as it rumbled into action. The vibrations of the bubbling water reminded her of that holiday in Iceland where Fred and she rather apprehensively sank into gurgling geezers, laughing as each of them accused the other of being the instigator of the eggy smell of sulphur all around them. They held hands then as always, never too old to appreciate the presence of the other one close by.

The steam from the kettle fogged her spectacles, enveloping her like an early morning mist. The tea soon soothed her as she gazed through the window into the garden where often deer would silently appear unannounced, innocent, and unaware. There had always been blackbird song in the lavender light of sundown, which most people wouldn't be aware of, but the garden had always been a true delight to Fred and her. That last summer had been hot and balmy but it was destined never to grow old and all too soon chevrons of birds had begun to head south making her yearn to journey along with them to escape the long dark days of winter ahead.

She returned to the suitcase; the familiar musky smells a reminder that it hadn't been used in many years. She carefully folded her newly laundered clothes neatly into the chasm of memories the old case held. She reminded herself of how many times she'd taken too many clothes on holiday, only to return with them clean in her suitcase, so this time she wanted to travel light and not take more than she would need. Tea leaves always calmed her nerves, so she'd take her special green tea with her, like on so many holidays before. She wandered through the house clearing the bathroom, collecting items to pack, and throwing others away. On the living room sideboard, she found a small battered frame holding their children's faces; she touched each one gently before she it slipped into her pocket. Her face came alive with a grin as she pictured how they used to play in the fairy ring at the end of the garden, being careful not to disturb the scattering of tiny mushrooms which were the fairies' houses. She often thought she could hear them still, playing in the garden in the quiet hours of the night. They were all grown now and no longer needed her, their visits becoming more and more sparce. In fact, it was her who needed them, but she didn't like to pester them with her problems. They had enough of their own in this brave new world.

She peered out at the naked poker-straight trees suspended in the first grip of winter. The early morning sun was watery, encapsulating the dew into webs of diamonds. It was a good time to go now, she thought. Finally packed, the cottage clean and she'd left a note for the postman. As she stepped into the garden her heart leapt. They had returned… the fairies. The ring was murky green like his green gaucho pants and filled with an array of tiny toadstools. She giggled and chastised them for staying away so long. Perhaps they knew that children would be coming here again soon, and the garden would become alive once more. She blew them a kiss goodbye. She'd had her fill of experiences, but she was sure there would be more to come, and a feeling of adventure invaded her senses once more. Excitement, yet sadness; unlike when he'd wrap his arm around her shoulders as they left. This time she would be travelling alone.

The Hospice bus was waiting; she knew they'd take care of her on this, her final holiday. The door closed quietly behind her.

About the author

Jeanne Davies has always enjoyed making up stories visiting other people's worlds and feelings, and began to submit to competitions a few years back. Seeing them in print is a huge encouragement and motivation. She's been fortunate enough to have short stories, flash fiction and poetry included in various anthologies and magazines, and her single author anthology *Drawn by the Sea* has recently been published by Bridge House.

The Little Statue

Christmas at the Cross Part II

Maeve Murphy

My Aunty Pat was avoided.

Everything around her was steeped in disapproval. When she rang up and spoke in her weird English Irish accent we all didn't want to talk to her. When I was a bad child, I was warned that I would end up just like her: pregnant, unmarried, who then gave away her child, went to London and went AWOL.

As I was walking out of the hospital, Santa passed me on his way in, carrying a sack of wrapped presents for the sick kids. As I hobbled slowly down the Euston Road back to the sin bin of St Pancras it did seem to me that I was now the living embodiment of Aunty Pat. Liked sex too much. Ruined because of it.

I got back to the flat, changed into my nightie, wrapped myself in rugs and blankets and sat beside the gas heater that was wafting heady gassy homicidal heat, but heat nonetheless. I sat there, staring into space. My eye fell on the wee statue Aunty Pat had given me. A tiny lead serene cross-legged Buddha. There was a knock at the door. I looked through the peep hole, terrified it might be Kieran. My now ex. It was in fact Nadina, laughing, holding a bag of potatoes. Nadina the prostitute from Kings Cross that I'd met just recently when she came begging at my door. She looked strange through the fish eye lens. She held up a bag of potatoes. I opened the door. Nadina thrust the bag into my hands.

"Thanks," I replied.

"Irish people like potatoes don't they?"

"We like blowing things up as well."

She laughed at the cultural stereotyping. Being London Asian she understood it was like me saying something about *Indians and curries*. She came in and sat down and spotted the pills sitting on the side table.

"What have you got?"

"A miscarriage."

She winced sympathetically.

"I've never had that."

"The bad luck's all mine."

She laughed.

"Heard it's woeful."

"I'll survive." I went back in and rearranged my blankets and rugs around me, repositioning myself nearer the gas fire.

"Do you want some potatoes?" She asked.

I nodded. I started to painstakingly heave myself up from the chair.

"I'll do it."

I wondered if I could trust her in the kitchen, but there really wasn't anything of value to nick, so I nodded. When the spuds were ready, she brought them in on two plates, all smashed up with a fork with a tiny bit of butter on top. In that moment, you know the spuds were actually the perfect thing. Totally delicious. Especially with the sprinkle of cumin and coriander spices on top. I was so happy in that moment, sitting with her, eating the spuds. She saw Rory's guitar in the corner, beside my bass and picked it up. She strummed it, then started to play and to sing softly. I was quite amazed. Her voice was so pure, so real, so deeply and honestly human, heart wrenching because of the level of anguish and love in her, it made me want to cry. She was singing about someone being a treasure. Simple but beautiful lyrics. With her black wild and matted mane and her pale black skin, her eyes so tightly shut, with the guitar in hands, her head tilting, sinking into the music, it was awesome, primal. I started to realise that this was quite an extraordinary woman. When she finished, I clapped.

"That was brilliant."

"Not bad for a slag," she joked in her husky London accent, taking out her tobacco and skins and rolling herself a cigarette. She stared at the guitar.

"Rory, the guy whose flat this is, owns that. Mine's that one." I nodded to the bass guitar.

"You can't play for a while." She looked at my bandaged hand. I nodded.

"We could start a band. Ladies of the night! What do ya think?" she said with playful glee.

It was a wild idea. But I liked it. "Great name!"

"Lots of creative people live here."

I nodded. They did. Broke ones.

"Where do you live?" I asked.

"Here. Next block." She laughed at what must have been my startled response.

"Who is the treasure you are talking about?" I asked.

"Me," she replied, matter-of-factly.

I felt moved. I wanted to know more but didn't want to pry. Instead she questioned me. "Your name means little flower in Gaelic."

"How did you know that?"

"You announced it in Burger King when we was all trying to help bandage your bleeding hand."

I laughed embarrassed remembering the chaos of the previous night.

"I was really drunk," I said.

"You were really something, not sure if it was drunk, you were ragin'."

155

She looked at me, creating the space for me to speak.

"I had met up with my ex."

"Why ex?"

"Well he is now. He started behaving badly, like with other women. I sort of pretended it wasn't happening. I thought maybe you shouldn't put restrictions on people..."

"Pleasing him, to win him over." She said smiling. I winced inside.

"And then, the other night, in Liverpool, he attacked me while I was sleeping."

She sat up, now listened carefully, with real heart, not phoney or hypocritical heart, or patronising or arrogant heart, or even hard heart, but real heart. She really heard me, which was amazing cos no one else seemed remotely interested.

"Where was he from?"

"Liverpool. Liverpool Irish, parents on both sides from Ireland."

"You thought familiar was safe."

"Yep... I also thought he was a bit of a hero, talking up for Irish people and young disadvantaged kids who get into crime. I thought he was really inspiring...."

"Had he been in prison?"

"Yeah, as a getaway driver for an armed robbery when he was very young."

"But turned bad in prison, a bit of a gangster?"

She was sharp.

"Not quite a gangster."

"Mates with. Probably how he got through prison."

I nodded. "Something like that." I was really only just waking up to all this.

"Anyway, I went to meet him, for a drink, cos he'd said he was sorry."

"Pleasing him." Nadina interrupted. I winced internally again.

156

"But then it all kind of exploded. I accidentally cut my hand." I continued.

She nodded taking it all in.

"What are you going to do in the New Year?"

"I dunno!" I shook my head laughing at the sudden topic change. "Do you know?"

"Probably the same. It's not that bad... I'm bidin' my time, bidin' my time, for Richard Gere to show up in his fancy car."

We both laughed hard at that.

"Actually I'm wanna get a demo done. Get a record deal. I just have to save a bit of money, then I'm going to live in Greece." She said everything with total confidence, totally convinced in her power. It was dazzling.

"But I dunno if I'd be able to handle the guys in suits, you know from record companies."

"You know how to handle guys."

She laughed giving me her cheeky grin. "We could both go to Greece, write songs! Then get a demo done. Do it that way round."

I loved her crazy enthusiasm. I told her, I didn't really know what I wanted except some structure in my life.

"You're a bit like the Buddha, left his palace on a quest."

I laughed, truly amazed she saw me like that.

"I had a thirst for more life, I dunno, adventure, something to grab me, electrify me, but I grabbed the wrong thing, Nadina. I fell in love with the wrong guy and I dunno maybe lost my fuckin' mind." I replied.

"This is spiritual," she insisted. "Let's see who gets enlightened first."

To see the two of us in our predicament, as if on a spiritual quest, was kind of crazy but also brilliant. She gave it meaning. She gave me hope.

"Do you want to keep hurting yourself, Blathnaid?"

I was startled at her directness.

"He's the one doing the hurting," I replied. She listened, said nothing, lit her cigarette and inhaled. As she exhaled, the smoke floated through the silence. I caught her eye. There was something in it.

"Tell me about your job?" I said, while trying to shake off a growing sleepiness. I wanted to listen to her. I wanted to know more about her. I really did.

Then there was a knock on the door. I jumped, she observed this.

"I'll get it." She got up.

"Thanks."

"I do it for the money," she replied as she got up.

"I'll help you hurt him if you want," she said casually as she crossed the room to go and open the door.

I could hear Mike's voice, my neighbour from downstairs.

"Is Blathnaid in? I was wonderin' if I could borrow a cup of sugar from her."

Rory had told me all about him in advance. Mike was from Dublin and a junkie.

But he was a good soul and someone not to be scared of. I had been a bit scared of him, but by now I knew Mike was alright.

"Yes, that's fine," I called out to him.

I got up from my seat and hobbled down the corridor to get the sugar for him.

"Are you okay?" Mike asked. "I saw you the other night."

"Yeah, yeah," I said. Making light of the ambulance that had come when I collapsed.

Mike stood there in his black canvas trousers, far too skinny, with his eyes peering out behind his strange pink tinted glasses. They made his eyes look a touch pink also. Made me think of a sick rabbit. He had jet black hair and a very strong Dublin accent. Mike handed me his cup for the sugar.

"Any news from Rory?"

"No, nothing, still travelling."

Mike was on methadone. He must have been the only junkie in the world who had never stolen, hard to believe I know, but the God's honest truth. He was so bloody soft, the only thing he had ever damaged was himself. He was also profoundly intelligent. Very curious about people. I had some quite interesting chats with him about "Ulysses". There is no doubt the Dublin working class are the most cultured in the world. And so polite also, always so courteous. Well he was.

"This is Nadina," I said.

As I went into the kitchen to get the sugar, I could hear him talking to Nadina about Hindu Gods, Shiva and Krishna, and about how he'd read in Hindu mythology that life in the world was maintained by Krishna's breathing. I liked the idea of the earth being inside this nice-looking Asian guy's lungs, expanding and contracting as he breathed in and out.

"What do you do?" I could hear Mike ask Nadina.

"Hand jobs for a tenner," she replied.

He laughed, clearly liking her spirit.

"I heard you singing, I thought you were a singer."

I joined them at the door and handed Mike the cup with sugar. I was now one of them. Outcasts, dregs of society. But in my eyes, in that moment, we were little urban shamans, not ruined or broken or even that hardened. People of humanity. Which as I increasingly realised was so fuckin' rare, anywhere. In that moment, I loved them both.

"You not going home then for Christmas?" asked Mike.

"No."

"Well Happy Christmas to you, Blathnaid."

"Thanks, Happy Christmas to you Mike."

"And to you Nadina." Mike added.

Nadina laughed sardonically.

After they left I wondered what Nadina had meant about helping to hurt Kieran.

I made myself a cup of tea and sat down again by the heater. I could hear Mike downstairs playing Velvet Underground and then talking to his dad on the phone and crying. He was telling him he loved him over and over. It was God awful to hear. I put an Etta James tape to block it out and lay down on the sofa to rest. She was singing about a Merry Christmas and receiving a diamond ring and how she was in paradise. I thought about Kieran, meeting him, in the bar where they played trad Irish music, the instant attraction, his good natured banter. The feeling for him hadn't disappeared. It was shoved aside by the terror and confusion from his recent attack. I must have fallen asleep on the sofa.

I had a horrible dream about crawling around on my hands and knees searching for a baby in a room full of children. I was in a bathroom, watching fluid go down a plug hole. I didn't want it to go down. Then there was the sound of really loud crashing in my dream.

I woke up shocked, to see Kieran standing in the doorway, staring at me. I screamed. But I also thought maybe I was still dreaming. But he was real.

"It's okay. I just want to talk to you… Get up and we'll have a cup of tea and a chat."

I nodded. His light chit chat felt surreal.

As I got up I saw that the front door had been kicked open and a guy with his back to me, was standing at the

160

unlit entrance. I turned to ask Kieran what was going on, when he suddenly hit me across the face with such force I went flying across the room, hitting the side of my cheek against the heavy wood junk table that the TV was on. Dazed I tried to get up to run out of the already blocked exit. But he pushed me down again and then crouching, put his hands round my neck area, sort of throttling me, banging the back of my head against the solid table. His mouth a line thin and the whites of his eyes widened. He looked crazy. I thought this was definitely death.

"Don't you fuckin DARE speak to me like that in front of people... do you hear me?" STUPID Bitch."

He got up to go, then turned to kick me one more time. I felt a surge of rage. Red hot rage streaming out of me. I didn't need Nadina to help me hurt him. Adrenalin pumping I grabbed his ankle, jerked it. I heard myself roaring, screaming. He lost his balance, landed on the floor, crashing his head. It didn't split or anything. I stared, shocked. Suddenly male arms were grabbing me, yanking me backwards. Must have been the guy at the door. I was trying to resist, kicking. Kieran, whose eyes were shut, was breathing. I twisted my head, to see who was holding me. It was his friend Nick from Newry who used to be in the IRA. I had mostly only met Kieran with his trendy mates and only dipped into his other reality a few times. More pounding noise, as two policemen came rushing into my sitting room. They asked what had happened? I didn't say anything. I couldn't say anything. I couldn't speak. I should have but I just couldn't. They saw the side of my face and the marks on my neck. Kieran got up from the floor.

"Whose flat is it?"

"Mine." I replied.

"You two are coming with us."

This was addressed to Kieran and Nick who nodded

strangely without protest. The policeman then told me to come down to the station in the morning to make a statement. Said I also needed to get the door fixed. Just like that it was all over.

I watched them out of the window, down on the street, with the blue light of the police car flashing, I could see them putting Kieran and Nick in the car.

I sat down on the sofa, dazed. I lit a cigarette and then another one, hands shaking. As the adrenalin started to wear off, I thought I might throw up. I wondered who'd phoned the police. I looked at the broken open door. Anyone could come in. The tiny lead Buddha Aunty Pat had given me caught my eye again. I didn't really like her the few times I met her but I thought the statue was beautiful. I put it in my pocket.

I crept down the stairwell in the dark and stopped outside David's flat. David was a guy I'd just met in the church soup kitchen when I'd gone to volunteer, who had the most deep brown eyes. I knocked on his door. He didn't answer. I knocked again, waited and was about to give up when the door opened.

"I'm on holiday abroad in a hot country."

"Someone broke into my flat, they've been arrested. But the door is broken… could I stay the night?"

It wasn't an easy thing to ask. His brown eyes were wary. It wasn't an immediate yes. He looked at my face which was red and really grazed. He nodded and I followed him inside.

"Want a cup of tea?"

"Yes please."

"Milk and sugar?"

"Yes, just one sugar. Actually two."

"I can make it three if you like"

I sank down on the dark red sofa in his sitting room while David went into the kitchen. I was amazed how well he'd done up his flat. It was practically luxurious in comparison to mine. Wooden floor, white painted walls, wooden box used as a coffee table, with two huge comfy sofas in a right angle facing a television. There were also some beautiful photographs of Africa on the wall.

He handed me a mug of tea.

"You do have a thing with the emergency services. Ambulance. Police. Got plans for the fire brigade?"

I laughed.

"Course you're used to that, what with the paras breaking down your door on a nightly basis. Living on the Falls Road, dodging the bullets. Standing in the rain at all those IRA funerals. In your black beret."

"I didn't live on the Falls Road."

He smiled nodding. He'd sussed that.

"What's going on? Is there some kind of axe murderer chasing you?"

"More like a psycho ex-boyfriend," I said as lightly as I could.

I noticed the poster of Leatherhead from slasher film *The Texas Chainsaw Massacre* on his wall. He clearly saw violence with an unreal film lens. He got up and went into another room and came out with some tissues and a tube of Savlon.

"You need to get an injunction, or go to a woman's refuge if you need a safe space."

The term women's refuge hit like a brick. I was in battered wife territory. Fuck. That's how he saw me. Fuck. That was a terrible place to be. Also this stay was clearly just for the evening. Emergency aid. Of course he was right – we didn't know each other.

"I'm going to go back to Belfast day after Boxing Day. Banks are open then."

"What so you can rob one?" He was a sarky fucker, but this time I did smile.

163

"So a cheque will have cleared by then."

"You're welcome to stay till then."

"Seriously thank you."

"How seriously dangerous is this guy?"

I didn't want to scare him. Truth is I didn't know.

"He doesn't know I'm here."

"You're welcome."

I caught his eye. This was huge of him. I felt exhausted. I could also now feel a throbbing pain in my cheek.

"I'm knackered."

He nodded.

"I'll show you the spare room."

I got up as he did and followed him, pointing out the bathroom and toilet on the way.

"Feel free to use the towels. I've just done a wash. So all clean."

He pointed to one towel in particular. I nodded. We carried on to the end of the passage. He opened the door. It was a little awkward and he was being formal to make it easier. I walked into his tiny spare room with a single bed and shelf with books on it. There were white walls and like a Mexican rug as a bed throw in vibrant bright yellow and red colour, a chair and a small mirror on the wall. He looked at me and smiled. He was still carrying the tissues and Savlon and handed them to me.

"Thanks. That rug Mexican?"

He nodded.

"Beautiful."

He went to go but stopped at the door. "Are you Okay?"

The compassionate gaze in his eyes pierced me, it was so different to his earlier dry detached tone. I couldn't really answer but I felt an overwhelming urge to nestle into him. It was purely instinctual as really he was practically a stranger.

He left. I closed the door. I looked at my face in the

164

mirror. Jesus. I looked a fuckin' wreck. My jelled up hair, sort of fluffy punky look was all flat. The side of my face was red, bright red near my eye. My black eyeliner looked wrong with the redness. I put a bit of the Savlon on my cheek. I lay down on the bed. Incredibly I slept.

I dreamt of a woman. She was being attacked by a man. She called out and a raging pack of dogs appeared. The man who then somehow had a stag's head on him fled, the dogs raced after him, hunting him. They caught up with him, attacking him viciously in a frenzy. Life went out of the man with the stag's head. The woman appeared with a bow and arrow, the dogs gathered round her, smiling she shot an arrow into the sky.

The bed room door opened. I woke, screamed. It was David, standing at the door in a red and white Santa hat. When I realised it was him, we both laughed in a kind of freaked out kind of way.

"Happy Christmas?!"

"Jesus Christ, you scared the shit out of me."

"So I did." He mimicked my accent.

"Shut up." I said not liking the mimicking. He laughed.

"I'm going round to my parents."

"I'm going to the police to press charges."

"Today? Christmas Day?"

I nodded.

"Well help yourself to coffee and toast. There is a fresh pot. No turkey I'm afraid."

"Coffee and toast is wonderful." I smiled.

"Spare key is on the table. See you later."

I nodded. "Thanks."

After breakfast, I walked down the side alley on my way to the police. It was deadly quiet. A woman with SAVED hand-written on her forehead walked towards me. She was wearing a denim mini skirt, high heels and was drunk or off her face on something.

She walked past singing "Oh Happy Day."

I was thinking of a witty quip.

"Blathanid." It was a northern Irish accent.

I turned. Walking towards me, was Nick, the ex IRA guy who'd broken into my flat with Kieran. I could smell a dirty rat coming. I felt like a really tight pressure against my skin as if it was stretched too tightly. He stopped in front of me.

"The peelers aren't following this up."

"What?"

"Kieran has decided not to press charges."

"What? What are you talking about?"

"He's not goin' to press charges."

I looked at him utterly incredulous.

"They've been let off with a police caution and the police have promised to keep a close eye on them. So you're safe."

"Keep a close eye on who?"

"That Paki brasser you've been hangin' out with and her pimp fella."

My jaw dropped. They were pinning this on Nadina and her pimp. How the hell did they make the connection between me and Nadina? So clearly their line was, Kieran had rescued me from King Cross scum who were breaking in and got roughed up in the process, but wasn't pressing charges. Nadina and pimp would also know whatever they say will not be believed, that's if they knew at all. An injunction needs police paperwork, and an intimidating "ex" IRA guy was telling me all this. Basically I was totally fucking snookered.

Nick looked at the marks on my face.

"I didn't realise they attacked you as well."

166

"Wise up. Kieran did that." I replied. "As you know."

A stare between us. He took out some money.

"How much for the door?"

"Fuck off."

He kind of laughed. A hard dry laugh.

I walked off. This was getting really scary. I walked around the block a couple of times, my mind buzzing on overload. I carried on walking and walking quickly and even quicker, round the block a few times more and found myself in the next courtyard, walking up the steps to Yoichi's flat. He was a local Japanese guy, who had spoken to me about karma. Now I had no appointment booked and it was Christmas day. But I knocked anyway and Yoichi opened the door, more than a touch surprised when he saw me. Nevertheless he gestured to me to come in. I walked inside. A woman in her late twenties was chanting to the scroll that Yoichi had hanging in his wooden cabinet. I sat down, a bit weirded out. I looked at the Buddhist scroll. It had bold black Chinese or Japanese characters written down the centre and smaller writing on either side. It was beautiful. Fresh.

"She'll finish soon," he told me.

Yoichi sat behind her and chanted with her. My squashed up mind, kind of expanded just listening to them. And then out of curiosity, I picked up the words and murmured the mantra with them. There was a lovely moment when the winter sun ray came in through the window and lit us all. It was like we were in deep harmony with all and each other.

After a while I felt my mind relax, the tight clench of anxiety, fear and hopeless rage loosened its grip. I felt space in my head that was free. I felt and found a state of happiness in my mind. Hard to explain. I had this happiness in me, tucked away, buried beneath the current relentless

167

terror treadmill. It was a bit like being high on dope, like that little pocket of happiness you hit. But this was natural, legal. I felt a loving feeling to everything. I could see me and what was happening and my heart opened to me. I felt a real compassion to me. I didn't need Nadina to get someone to hurt Kieran. I didn't have to hurt him either. I just felt I didn't want my own life hurt anymore. This was a warm loving spacious feeling. Not tight. Goodness had not left my world. And I wanted to give that goodness also.

The woman finished chanting and turned round to look at me. She was smiling and had such an alive vibrant presence; I could feel her energy. She was Italian.

"I got here late to see Yoichi. Maybe it meant we could meet on time!"

I laughed. "Divine timing!"

She smiled.

"I support the young women locally. What happened your face?"

"Psycho ex-boyfriend," I joked. I did a cartoon-like mock punch to my face.

She laughed, liking my black humour.

"Did you walk into a wall?" she asked. I realised she hadn't quite taken it in.

"No. Actually him or his mate kicked the door in."

She didn't laugh this time. "I'm Rita."

I nodded. I liked her Italian accent.

"What's your name?"

"Blathnaid, means little flower."

"Out of the muddy swamp the Lotus flower blooms."

"So we can get out of the swamp of Kings Cross?" I said joking.

"We can get out of our lowest life state, bring out our Buddha state."

"Yeah, I think I felt it… beautiful."

I looked at Yoichi. He was putting mince pies on a plate. He had his silver Christmas tree with fairy lights on in the corner. It was bonkers; he had way more Christmas decorations than anyone else's flat I'd been in.

"Happiness not Holiness."

Yoichi clapped his hands in delight. I'd got it.

"Happiness in you, all time. *And* can get out of the Kings Cross, anytime!" Yoichi said this with a warm smile. He had such clear joyful eyes. He offered me a mince pie. I took it.

"What do you do Yoichi?"

"I work in a Sushi restaurant on Eversholt Street."

I nodded. Yoichi could see my fascination.

In my mind, Buddhas were eastern male monks in orange robes who meditated in hill top monasteries. I thanked them both and left. I felt a lot better. A lot clearer too. Outside it was snowing. Kind of magical Christmas Day stuff. But as I was walking through the courtyard, my heart seized up as through the falling snow I saw Kieran walking towards me. He stopped, casually blocking my path. There were some picnic tables in the courtyard, so I indicated we sit there. I wanted to stay in public. I could smell booze off him.

"Your mate Mike told me you had a miscarriage."

So it was Mike. He was the one who told Kieran about Nadina also. Probably rang the police as well.

"When did you speak to Mike?"

"Last night, I came back, to see if you were okay."

I felt sick. This was enough. I'd had enough.

"You weren't there."

I shook my head. Careful not to say a word.

"I didn't know you were pregnant. You didn't tell me... why didn't you tell me?"

"I wasn't hundred percent aware of it myself. Very early on. But I thought I did say."

He looked at me, with a hint of concern. "I'm going to rent a place for the New Year in Brighton. You could come and stay for a few days. Rest."

I shook my head. "It's enough."

I took out the little lead Buddha that Aunty Pat had given to me; it was still in my pocket from the previous night. I stared at it. I wanted that peace. I leant across and gave it to him. The attachment, the invisible chord whatever it was tying us, broke.

He picked it up, looked at it carelessly then got the seriousness of my gaze. Then I just got up and walked away. He called my name once, but not twice. Maybe he felt it was enough also, but to be honest I was still fearful I might hear his footsteps behind me.

I kept on walking. Kind of exhilarated. I looked round a few times, to check, but he wasn't behind me. I felt strong. I'd changed. Maybe I'd even changed my karma. It was still snowing. But I didn't feel any cold. I kept walking all the way to Covent Garden. No one was around. The shops were closed. I found myself a quiet spot in Neal's Yard, under a droopy snowy tree. This had been a shit Christmas but I forced myself to think about next year, my future.

It was on the way back, I was still mulling everything over, what I was going to do, how I would do it, until when I reached the top of Midhope Street I saw the police and tape across the road and an ambulance outside the building I lived in. Someone was screaming. The girlfriend of the New Zealand artist appeared out of the building, hysterical. Horrified, I then watched as Mike was taken out, he looked dead.

But nothing prepared me for what I saw next. Everything went into slow motion as I witnessed Kieran carried out on a stretcher, bright red blood splattered across his white shirt. He looked unconscious. I stared, not able to let what I saw connect to the reality of what was there. I became vaguely aware of David coming running towards me. Everything was muffled. Kieran, he said, had been stabbed multiple times with a broken bottle.

David told the police I lived there and they let me through.

I went back to David's in a daze. We sat, unable to speak. My mind was jangled, jumbled.

I looked at David; he was really jangled also. "What thoughts are going on underneath that elusive surface?"

"Just glad it was that way round," he replied.

It was still snowing softly outside.

I thought about the little statue.

I thought about Aunty Pat. I wondered if maybe she wasn't so bad.

There was a knock on the door. "Police."

David opened the door. Two policemen walked inside. They interviewed us quickly and left. It came on the news as they were going. A man in hospital after a stabbing incident in Kings Cross. Another man dead from an overdose. The implication was that one had stabbed the other then killed himself. An argument, a brawl that had got out of control.

I wept.

I also felt a colossal relief.

I could breathe.

For now… Released.

David heated up some plum pudding he'd brought back from his mum's.

He asked me if I'd like some, I agreed.

We ate it hopefully and watched *White Christmas* with Bing Crosby on TV.

About the author

Maeve Murphy is an award winning writer-director from N.Ireland. Her first feature, *Silent Grace*, was critically acclaimed and chosen as the UK entry for Cannes and chosen for The Irish Times film critics' "Best 50 Irish Films Ever Made". Her second feature *Beyond the Fire* screened at ICA and on BBC2. Her third, *Taking Stock*, a festival award winning comedy caper starring Kelly Brook was released in cinemas across the UK and "popular on Netflix." Maeve has had articles published in national newspapers, and her debut short story *Christmas at the Cross* was published by Bridge House in their 2019 anthology *Nativity* and in the Irish Times *12 stories at Christmas*. Her new film about Shane MacGowan and Victoria Mary Clarke is in development. *Christmas at the 'Cross,* her debut novella/ single author collection, will be published by Bridge House in 2021, and Maeve has also received a draft screenplay award from Screen Ireland to adapt it.

www.maevemurphy.net/

The Perfect Haven

Janet Howson

This need to escape, this need to disconnect and somehow find myself again was taking over my every thought. How could I find the necessary solitude, a space to breathe away from family, friends and work colleagues? I felt anxious, restless, claustrophobic and trapped in my own anxiety. I needed a cure and I think, at last, I had found it.

The website was encouraging. I liked the play on words. "There is no need to 'mull over' the decision on whether to visit the Isle of Mull." It made me smile. Something I hadn't done in a long while.

It then went on to describe the attraction of the Island. White sandy beaches, swimming in the North Atlantic, the colourful harbour of Tobermory, small villages dotted around the coast offering a peaceful haven. It suggested bird watching, glamping and appreciating the sealife: puffins, seals, ducks and otters. It described it as a geological wonder.

It all sounded perfect. I read on further, absorbing and delighting in the detail. It was the fourth largest Scottish island. It was a forty-five minute crossing on a ferry from Oban on the West coast of Scotland to Craignure on Mull. You needed to book six weeks in advance. I needed immediacy. This was too long ahead I couldn't think that far in advance. However, from Fishniss, further North up the coast, it was a twenty minute crossing and you couldn't book. You just turned up and waited. That suited me far better.

I would just go. Put a few essentials in a bag. I wouldn't need bedding. The glamping sites would provide that. I would have my car, my smart phone for Google maps, some cash, my bank cards, myself.

I read again from the website. "A perfect Scottish Island for a short vacation away from the cities. A perfect haven. Mull can lay claim to some of the most varied scenery of the Inner Hebrides. Noble birds of prey soar over mountains and coasts while the western waters provide good whale watching." I felt myself absorbed into the beauty of it all before I had got there. The decision had been made. I was going.

Once it became a reality I felt energy returning. That feeling of a future, something to look forward to. At the back of my mind there were unanswered questions, ones I didn't want to think about in my present mood. Do I let my family Know I was going away? Do I tell them I am going but not where? Do I leave instructions for work? Do I confide in my loyal friend, the friend I had told everything to since we met on our first day at secondary school? The questions were there but I buried them deep in my psyche.

I glanced in the mirror and adjusted my headscarf. I had rejected the idea of wearing a wig. I had tried one, but it was itchy and uncomfortable so I returned to the colourful headscarves, presents mainly from family and friends eager to help, eager to please. Perhaps I would change my mind about the wig later.

I felt I wanted to hurry now. I wanted to be there. I knew I had a long drive so the sooner I set off the better. I could always sleep in the car if time ran out for the ferry. Then I would be there for the first crossing in the morning. I had a blanket in the car. I would take food and water, a flask, a pillow. I didn't want to write a list. I didn't want to be that organised. I had always been so organised.

It didn't take long. Boiling the kettle, stuffing a few clothes into a bag. Removing a pillow from the spare bed, a bed slept in by my daughter on her return home weekends from university. The pillow smelt of her perfume. What was the name of it?

I had filled the car up with petrol recently. I put the post code of the ferry terminal on the satnav. Was I really doing this? Excitement filled my body, a queasiness in my stomach, a light headiness. I turned on the ignition.

It became a reality as soon as I heard my request at the dock for the ferry, "A single ticket to Mull, please." Then realising with a guilty pang what I had asked for, "Sorry, I meant a return." The heat from my body rose to my face. I mustn't panic. I must stay calm. Push aside the guilt. Forget responsibilities. They could all manage without me. I would return refreshed, renewed and ready.

Once we had left the dock and I was parked on board and had climbed the stairs to get to the deck and was leaning over sitting on a bench with the wind whipping round my body, a cup of steaming hot coffee in my hand, I felt a cleansing process. The sea lapping against the boat's sides, the cries of the seagulls, the miles of nothing, just sky and water. The chemotherapy, the hospital appointments, the sickness, the fatigue were all behind me. I felt free. I could disown it. No one would be asking the same well-meant and concerned questions. "How are you feeling?" How's the treatment going?" "How are the family taking it?"

The first thing that struck me on my first view of the island was how green everything was. The rocky peaks and green slopes of the Mull mountains. Even the trees and the grass all seemed much greener than the mainland. I then was entranced by the crofts and the houses surrounded and protected by the Mull landscape. I loved it. I always knew I would love it.

I didn't want to be in my car for long. I wanted to walk, feel and absorb these new surroundings. I had Googled a glamping site and set off with an urgency, intent in ridding myself of all the reminders of civilisation I wanted to leave behind.

Before long I was free. I breathed in deeply and shut my eyes. It was cold, but I didn't care. I felt it was a curative process, like a cold bath or a cold compress on an aching limb. I faced the sea, and spread my arms out in a crucifix pose and listened to the noises created by nature. I opened my eyes in time to see a beautiful eagle swooping around the cliffs, his majestic being was both impressive and threatening. Then with a dive he had plucked a fish from the sea and was flying off, triumphant, holding securely to the catch with his talons.

I walked and I walked and I walked. The miles tired but invigorated me. Then it overwhelmed me. A wonderful sense of relaxation brought about by the exercise and the power of my surroundings. My mind was emptying, deleting and calming.

I lay on the grass, facing the hazy, blue sky and smiled. It was all going to be fine. This is what I needed. I had chosen the right environment to become completely healed. The advert was right. Why would you need to mull over a decision to come here? It was absolutely perfect.

About the author

Janet taught English and drama in comprehensive schools in Redbridge, Havering and Essex for 35 years. She has always loved the written word and reads about three novels a month. When she was retired she eventually joined a writer's group, meeting published writers and attending workshops and listening to talks from authors. She started to write short stories and loved the experience and now some of these have been published. Her first novel *Charitable Thoughts* was published on March 31st 2020. She has also been published in various anthologies, the latest being *It Happened in Essex*, tall tales from the Basildon Writers' Group, all proceeds going to Basildon Hospital Radio.

The Sound of Love

Stuart Larner

"You ask what is the sound of love? I'll tell you, Roberto. For me, it is the sound of our mother being shot. By Franco's troops up there in the olive grove. She was trying to protect us and save our father. The whole village heard it. A loud single crack. Franco hoped it would be an example. The sound of fear. But we all knew it was the sound of love."

His sister's words echoed in his memory as Roberto fingered the family photograph from eighty years ago. He hadn't seen this photograph until he had visited his estranged elder sister recently just before she died.

"Franco's men had come for her. They said she was a revolutionary. They wanted her to tell them where our father was. But she wouldn't. She picked you up and ran down the lane with you. I tried to follow, but an aunt held me back. They captured Mother and took her away to a sham trial. Aunt Carmen took us both in, but later I was sent further away to Aunt Isabel.

"This photograph was taken just two years before then. Happier times. You used to play on mother's lap with that red rattle that had a pony on it. She kept it hidden deep in the front pocket of her apron to see if you could find it just by the shape and the sound amongst the folds. You used to chuckle when you found it. You had such a mischievous laugh."

Roberto brought the photograph to his lips and kissed it, then put it back in his bedside drawer.

He looked out through their Spanish farmhouse bedroom window, squinting at his meadows dotted with sheep. He could just make out that one sheep had separated herself from the flock. It was too far away to be sure, but he guessed it was his favourite one with the black eye patch and twisted ear.

"Roberto," his wife Angela broke into his reverie from the bedroom doorway. Her serious face with its jet-black hair, dark olive skin and penetrating gaze suggested she tended to adopt a realistic attitude to life.

She sighed and shook her head. "You shouldn't dwell so much on the past. Come and eat your supper."

When he had sat down at the table in the kitchen with its oak beams and blue-and-white tiled walls, Angela brought the rabbit and garlic casserole from the log-fired oven.

"I've noticed a change in you," she said. "You've been so quiet these last few days. Is it the news?"

"Yes. Have they found any bodies yet?"

"I think so. The university announced it on the radio whilst you were out in the top pasture."

"I'm finding it very difficult to come to terms with all of it." He helped himself to potatoes and asparagus. "I want to know what really happened to her on that day, and whether she actually is buried up there in the mass grave in the olive trees."

"It's so difficult to get any answers from mass graves," she said. "Often those bodies cannot be identified after eighty years. You will only upset yourself by inquiring."

"No. It is my mother. I owe her that."

"You hardly knew her. Only a couple of years old when she died."

"Perhaps they can use DNA testing," said Roberto in hope.

"Don't stress yourself. It will lead nowhere."

"But I have the photograph…" He sniffed back a tear.

"Eat your supper. I don't want to see you upset."

Roberto had been thinking about this for days. He alternated between wanting to see his mother's skeleton in the mass grave, and fearing that it would be sacrilege. Indeed, it sometimes occurred to him that the university was prying into people's private lives just for the sake of someone's research job.

None of this seemed to interest his grandson, Pedro, who was spending a few days from college and his father's business to help Roberto repair fences. To Pedro this was something that had happened a long time ago and was best forgotten about.

One night, as he sat drinking his bedtime brandy, Roberto told them that he thought the mass grave was a place of national importance, and should be preserved.

Angela sighed. "If you go up there too early and see the grave before they close it and make it into a shrine, then the sight of it might disturb you. Knowing you, it could worry you a lot."

"Franco had a decent burial," retorted Roberto. "Laid in state in a mausoleum. Why him, and not my mother? We have a family plot."

During that night, he awoke and went to the bathroom. After coming back to bed, he lay tossing and turning for half an hour, unable to get to sleep.

Eventually in the darkness Angela, who had also awoken, ventured a quiet, "What's the matter?"

"I dreamt about my mother. For the first time ever in my life, I could see her clearly."

The next day he rang up the archaeology site and fixed an appointment for the afternoon of the day after.

On the day of the appointment, after Pedro had set off back to college, Roberto and Angela tucked into a breakfast of coffee, sliced ham, bread and black olives.

"Roberto, I have looked into your DNA idea," said

Angela slowly. "It would cost five thousand Euros each one, and they are not always successful. They would have to do them all, and if there were a hundred there then it could cost half a million. They're not paying for it, and we don't have the money. On top of that, if you want her remains exhumed and reburied in the family plot it would cost so much more on top. It would be very hard to get any funding. We're hand to mouth here on the farm as it is. I'm sorry, but that's it."

Roberto's face fell. There was a long silence and then he said sorrowfully, "Well then, I suppose I'll have to accept the fact that it can't be done." He added with a feeling of relief that comes from long-resisted acceptance, "All right. I won't think about it anymore. I won't go to the site."

After breakfast, he took his sheepdog and went in the Land Rover to check on the flock in the northern pasture. There had been talk in the village of a stray dog that had been worrying sheep.

At the top of the field, he looked back down over the hillside to the farmhouse with its white walls and red-tiled roof, the two stables for the horses and the almond trees, and wondered how Pedro would fare when he inherited all this.

Then he noticed an object in a corner of the field. As he got closer, he saw that it was a dead ewe. Its throat had been savaged, and its body half-eaten. Normally he would bring fresh carcases down to barbecue and feed to the dogs. But, as he looked at its black eyepatch and branding he recognised it as his favourite that had given birth last year.

As he stared at the ewe, something made him feel that he should do something for her. He had not been there in the final moments when it had been savaged by the stray dog, and he felt that he had let her down. He took a spade from the Land Rover, dug a grave, and buried it. Afterwards, he decided to give her a name. Anastasia, meaning 'Resurrection'.

When he drove back down and told Angela, she said, "That's what happens in Nature. You should have brought it down to barbecue and feed the dogs. Some creatures are just born to give birth and die."

He stiffened and glared at her. "Is that what you think? Just born to give birth and die? The ewe was a mother!"

In that moment he realised that he would have to keep the appointment. He knew that it might bring him nothing but misery, yet something was telling him to go.

On arrival at the site, he saw large mounds of earth obscuring his view beyond a wire fence.

"We can't allow you to view the actual graves," said the young woman in a white coat. She was wearing glasses and her black hair was in a ponytail. "But we can show you some of the coins that we found, if you'd like to come into the cabin."

"Well, even if they were my mother's coins, then at least I will have had contact, and I will feel better."

"We cannot say that they were any particular person's. We've only people's reports at the time that your mother might have been buried here. Her body could be somewhere else."

She led him into the cabin, put on a pair of white gloves, and provided him with a pair.

"These are some of the coins we have found so far. Note they are an assortment from the early part of the twentieth century."

She carefully handed him each coin, meticulously pointing out the denomination and year of minting. He soon got bored with the monotonous anonymity of the everyday objects, finding no guarantee of a link with anyone.

181

"This is something else we have also found," she said, opening a box, and taking out a small red object caked in mud. "We think this dates from between 1930 and 1940. Made of celluloid, there seems to be a picture of a pony on one side. Our investigation is still in progress."

Cradling it in her hands, she offered it into his.

His heart leapt as the small movement caused the object to rattle.

The sound of love.

About the author

Stuart Larner is a chartered psychologist. He has research papers, articles, stories, poems, and the books *Guile and Spin*, *The Car*, and, as Rosy Stewart, *Hope: Stories from a Women's Refuge*.

His plays have had rehearsed readings and performances in York and Scarborough.

He has stories in Bridge House anthologies:
 A Real Gem (Baubles, 2016);
 Pictures at an Exhibition (Glit-er-ary 2017);
 The Flaw (Crackers 2018).

See his blog. https://stuartlarner.blogspot.com/p/stuff-you-can-access-now.html

and website https://slarner5.wixsite.com/hope

The Tangle of the Isles

Elizabeth Cox

As she drew up at the ferry port in Oban, Norma looked at the clock on the dashboard of her Peugeot. Twenty to twelve. She had two hours to wait before the ferry set sail for Mull. She would rather it was ten hours or better still not at all. She rifled through her bag discarding used tissues and lipsticks haphazardly onto the striped seat in search of her ferry ticket. Triumphantly she extracted it from the debris on the seat and placed it on the dashboard.

In the bottom of her handbag, she discovered the remains of the screwed-up letter she had received which brought her to this place. It was very pink and scented, and she held it to her nose. So typical of Catherine – always over the top with everything. She inhaled, but only smelled the acrid scent of betrayal, not the scent of roses.

Why she had been sent an invitation to her sister's silver wedding party, she could not imagine. She hadn't been home here to Mull in over ten years. Since her mother's funeral to be exact, and she had never thought to be here again. She had finished with Mull, and Mull had released its hold on her with the passing of her mother.

She shoved all her belongings back into her shabby leather DKNY tote bag bought a few years ago with the proceeds of a particularly lucrative job and got out of the car. Carefully locking the vehicle, she breathed deeply. That familiar smell of oily sea water mixed with sharp salt assailed her nostrils. Even with the aroma of engine oil, the air was still fresher than at home in Manchester. The jumbled houses surrounding the harbour were reflected in the still waters and beyond were the heather covered hills of the Highlands. Moored alongside the trawlers and

183

pleasure boats alongside the dock was the ferry, its familiar red funnels blazing in the autumn sun. There was just a short stretch of water between her and the past. Did she have the courage to cross it? She shook her head to bring herself back to the present and her dark curls released themselves from the pearl hair clip which were keeping them in order. She realised that she just had time to find herself a sandwich before the boat sailed.

She turned right, away from the quayside towards a small café she remembered. When she arrived there, she found it was now a vape shop. Stamping her foot in frustration, she walked along a cobbled alley and turned into a square. In the corner there was a café. She realised she did not have much time now. It would have to be a take-away drink and sandwich. Today was not going well. Hopefully it wasn't an omen of what was to come. She was served by a pleasant girl with big blue eyes and a cheery smile.

"I'll have a smoked salmon sandwich on wholemeal," she ordered glancing up at the chalked menu on the blackboard, "and a cappuccino. Sorry, please," she added when she saw the girl's face.

"No problem, madam, just a moment." The girl turned towards the counter to prepare her order. Norma closed her eyes for a moment, taking in the hissing and chugging of the coffee machine and the chattering of the other customers who were sitting companionably at the small wicker tables. The girl returned and handed her a brown paper bag containing her food and drink.

"Thanks," she grunted ungraciously and turned away. From the corner of her eye she could see the girl pulling a face at her fellow server. She felt sorry then. She shouldn't take her problems out on the young woman. "Thank you very much," she reiterated and gave the girl a big smile. She was rewarded with an even bigger one from the girl and her companion. Cheered by this brief encounter she walked briskly back to her car. The exhilarating breeze coming off the sea cleared her mind, and she began to look forward to the upcoming journey.

When she returned, they were beginning to load the cars. She drove on to the ferry and parked her car in the allotted space, then made her way up onto the deck. The whistle hooted and the ship began to make its way from its berth onto the open sea. As Oban became more distant, Mull began to loom large in the distance. It only took forty minutes to Craignure from the mainland and Norma counted every one of them. Once she docked in Craignure, it would take her around another twenty minutes to drive to her home village of Salen. Norma had booked herself into a local B&B, where she could rest before contacting her family. That would happen all in good time. When she was ready.

She drew up at the house fully aware that she had been watched, as she drove through the village. It was a very quiet place and out of season not many strangers were seen. Oh well here goes, she thought as she stepped out of the car drawing her cashmere scarf up around her face. She took her bag from the boot and before she could knock on the door it was flung open by a plump grey-haired woman wearing a well-washed lilac jumper and tweed skirt.

"Welcome dearie, do come into the warm. It's quite chilly now the sun's gone down." The soft accents of the local dialect threw Norma and she began to tear up, even though she was irritated by the familiarity of the greeting. She rubbed her eyes with the scarf pretending it was the wind which had made her eyes water. "You must be Miss McLean. Your room's ready for you, but would you like a cup of tea first before you go up?"

185

Grateful for the woman's prattling, Norma allowed herself to be led into the cosy lounge and took a seat in a deep tartan armchair close to the roaring fire. She sunk into it and closed her eyes letting the warmth seep into her cold bones.

"Here you are Miss McLean, I hope you like scones. It's my own raspberry jam too. I'm sorry I forgot to introduce myself, I'm Mrs Henderson. When you've had your tea, I'll show you to your room." She placed the tea tray on the low table and left Norma to her own devices. After she'd gone, Norma realised that she had not uttered a word herself in that exchange and chuckled. The teapot was dressed in a knitted tea cosy, lilac like its owner's jumper, and Norma was reminded of her mother's kitchen and all those teas after school. After she had eaten the delicious warm scones and drunk the tea, she looked around unsure what to do next. Then she spotted a bell on the bookshelf and rang it. Mrs Henderson appeared like the genie from the bottle brandishing a wooden key fob and some clean towels. Before Norma could open her mouth, Mrs Henderson took charge.

"This way dearie. I've already taken your bag upstairs. I've given you the room with a view towards the sea. I hope you'll be comfortable. Have you visited Mull before, dearie? You look familiar." The woman narrowed her eyes and peered into Norma's face.

Norma realised that all this time Mrs Henderson had been summing her up, the very thing she hadn't wanted to happen.

"No, I haven't been a visitor before." She was aware that this was only a half-truth, if not a downright lie and felt badly about it but didn't want to have to elaborate on her relationship with the island.

"No. Well I could have sworn I'd seen you before. Breakfast is from eight to nine. Enjoy your stay." Mrs

Henderson thrust the key fob into Norma's hand and turned on her heel.

Norma could tell the woman was miffed. She hadn't wanted to make an enemy so soon. In such a small place she knew she couldn't hide; Mrs Henderson would be reporting on her existence in every shop in the village and on every street corner. She would have to contact Catherine soon. But not tonight.

She was hungry, but all she needed was sleep. It had been a long day with the drive from Manchester. She poked in the hospitality tray and found some shortbread biscuits which she began to unwrap. Then she remembered she had only eaten half of her sandwich and rummaged in her bag. She could have a good breakfast in the morning.

She lay awake for some time, listening to the distant pounding of the sea and the call of screech owls flying across the night punctuated by the squeak of some unlucky rodent. These were the sounds she remembered.

She was awoken by the rattling of rain against her window, a reminder she was in the Western Isles. She drew the curtains back and saw that it was just getting light. She checked the time – 6.30. Still a bit early. Even when she was showered and dressed, it would not be time for breakfast. She wondered if there were any other guests.

She sat on the bed and arranged her papers around her with the scented letter at the centre. *Catherine and Dougal invite you.* Why would they after what they had done to her? They hadn't spoken to each other since her mother's funeral and that had been tense – only necessary words exchanged. Still after breakfast she would have to contact them before they found out from others that she was there. They'd never had any children and Norma always wondered why. It was never a subject broached between the sisters, even when they were talking.

187

When the clock in the hallway chimed eight o'clock, Norma ventured down to the dining room where she was met by a frosty Mrs Henderson. The barest pleasantries were exchanged, and breakfast ordered. Norma glanced around the room. Hers was the only table set for breakfast. There were the usual pats of butter and pots of homemade jam and marmalade on the table. The end table was laid with fruit and breakfast cereals, so she helped herself. Mrs Henderson returned with a pot of coffee and some toast slammed on the table. When she came back with Norma's cooked breakfast, she lingered.

"You lied to me last night." she said. "I knew I'd seen you before – or someone like you. James McKay was on the boat yesterday, and he recognised you. He said you were Mrs McLean's eldest daughter. God rest her soul."

"I am. I didn't want to be recognised, before I had chance to see my sister. She doesn't know I'm coming, it's a surprise."

The woman brightened up. "Oh, you can rely on me, dearie. I won't tell anyone. I don't know about Jamie though he's a bit of an old woman, you know."

Norma did know. It was because of him that this situation had arisen in the first place. Him and his big mouth.

She thanked Mrs Henderson for her delicious breakfast, glad to have the woman back on side. Returning to her room, she picked up her phone and smoothing down the invitation letter she dialled the number she found on it. The phone rang twice – she terminated the call before anyone could answer. She'd call later, that would be better. She'd go for a walk now, see what had changed in the village. She took her coat from the hanger, she shrugged into it and wrapped her scarf around her face. The winds could be fierce around here.

She pulled the door quietly behind her and stepped out onto the neat path. She filled her lungs with the abrasive salty scent of the sea. The wind made her eyes water. It must be the wind. As she walked down the familiar streets, her mind was working overtime, remembering, going over old hurts. Although she had just had breakfast, she pushed open the blue-painted door of the Copper Kettle – the only coffee shop in town. Inside, she slid into a seat close to the window, so she could watch the comings and goings in the street. A young girl came over to her table. "What would you like?" she asked with a smile.

"Just a latte please," Norma answered glancing up at the girl. "What's your name?"

"I'm Joanna and I'm your server today," the girl answered as she walked away towards the counter.

With a jolt Norma realised the impersonal reply emphasised the loneliness she experienced in her daily life. No family only work friends, no special person in her life. She had been successful but at what cost. Time would tell.

The girl came back with her coffee and a complimentary biscuit. Norma scraped two spoons of sugar out of the bowl and stirred it into her cup. The coffee shop began to fill up. Friends meeting each other, harassed mothers with small children, old age pensioners out for a weekly treat, they all took their usual Saturday places. They belonged. Joanna came up to her.

"Can I get you anything else, Madam?" she asked, obviously concerned at the time Norma had taken up the table.

"No thanks, Joanna, I'll be leaving now." Gathering up her scarf and bag, she scrabbled in her purse for a pound coin which she left on the saucer. She scraped her chair back and made her way through the crowd waiting for a table, apologising as she stood on a woman's foot and made a child wail simultaneously.

189

It was no good. She would have to make that phone call. She found an old seat beside the sea and looked out at the horizon. It was so beautiful, even though it was windy, and the waves were angry bashing and crashing their white foam on the seaweed covered rocks. The sea was a winter grey reflecting the gusting clouds in the sky. She realised, she had missed her home, but she was here now.

She dialled the number again and waited for the call to be answered this time.

"Hello." The soft voice was so familiar, she thought she might cry. "Who is this?"

"Is that Catherine?"

"Yes. Is that you Norma? I'd know your voice anywhere even though we haven't spoken for years." Trust Catherine to get one in, Norma thought before answering. Memories of her sister came flooding back. Catherine, always the abrasive one, always avoiding the blame. She sighed.

"Yes, it's me. I thought I would take you up on your invitation. I couldn't resist seeing Dougal and you twenty-five years on." If Catherine could get one in, so could she.

"That's so good. I've missed you. I can't wait to see you. Where are you?"

Norma was rather taken aback at the warmth in her sister's voice. She gulped. "I'm, I'm sitting on a seat overlooking the sea."

"You're here? You must come up to the house. You know where we live." Norma realised sadly she didn't know where her sister lived. "We live in the old farmhouse on the Craignure road, you know the old Mackay place. We bought it when the old man died. We've done it up since then. No more smelly cows and mud. Remember when we used to play there with Rory?"

Norma remembered. That's when she first fell in love

with Dougal. They had been teenagers together– her and Dougal, Catherine and Rory until Norma went away to the mainland for university. Things changed then.

"Yes, yes I remember. You and Rory were really sweet on each other for a while, weren't you?"

"We were, until he decided he preferred Janet."

"And that's when you decided you wanted my Dougal." Norma couldn't help it coming out of her mouth and regretted it as soon as it was said. There was silence on the other end of the phone. Oh she'd blown it now, she thought, but Catherine answered. Her voice was breaking.

"Please come up to the house."

Norma swallowed hard. "I'm on my way," she said. She knew the way. Each step was familiar, each footstep placed in one that had gone before. The clouds began to part, and a weak sun streamed through the clouds lighting a path across the sea. She had driven past their house on the way from the ferry and had not known her sister lived there. She walked briskly buffeted by the wind from the ocean, but she soon found herself outside their front door. She hesitated. The door was flung open and there stood her sister surrounded by two boisterous dogs as usual. Catherine had changed. The bubbly blonde woman she had known was transformed. Catherine's hair was prematurely grey, her face was haggard, and she was using a walking frame. This was her younger sister. Norma tried to hide her reaction, but it was too late. Catherine had seen the horror which had passed across Norma's face. She smiled sadly.

"Come in Norma, you're so welcome." Norma wrapped her arms around her sister and held her close. "Things have changed, as you can see."

They went into the house preceded by the dogs. "That's Paddy and that's Nancy," Catherine said pointing to each dog in turn. "They're mad things. Go lie in your beds, horrors!" The dogs slunk off into the kitchen.

191

"They're lovely, Catherine. You always did love dogs. I remember when you said you wanted a house full of dogs and no children."

"Yes, sadly we had no children." Catherine turned her face away from Norma and gazed into the distance.

To cover her embarrassment, Norma concentrated on the contents of her handbag.

"Nice bag Norma," Catherine reached out to touch the soft leather of the handbag. "Did you get it through your work?"

"Yes, it was a sample," Norma replied feeling she had to justify the high-end purchase. "Catherine, what has happened to you?" Her voice was barely a whisper.

"Oh, I'm OK you know. I had a stroke a year ago. I know, I know I'm too young, but it's happened now, and we need to make the best of it. I was in hospital for a couple of months." Catherine shrugged and pulled a face at her sister. "I got most things back but my walking's not great, as you can see." She gestured towards the walking frame. "We get by."

"Why did no one let me know? I could have helped – got you some treatment – visited." Norma's voice tailed off.

"We weren't talking remember."

"I'm sorry for that now, but I did feel betrayed when you married Dougal – my boyfriend." Norma looked Catherine straight in the eye. "Very betrayed."

"I'm sorry too, but you didn't want him. You never came home, hardly ever phoned him. The man was lonely."

"He could have come to see me in Edinburgh. He was invited often enough. Where is he by the way?"

"He's gone to Tobermory to get some things for the party tonight. He'll be back soon." Catherine glanced out of the window, as if wishing her husband to appear outside. The girls sat in silence for a few minutes not sure what to say next. Norma cast her eyes around the humble sitting room, taking in the faded pink wallpaper.

Catherine visibly brightened when she heard the key in the lock. "Here he is now."

Norma did not turn around when she heard the sitting room door open.

"Hello darling, you OK. I got the stuff you asked for. Oh sorry, I didn't realise you had a visitor." Dougal went to turn away towards the kitchen.

His voice penetrated Norma's heart. She heard its familiar warm tones and remembered gruffness, and for a moment she was transported to another place and another time.

"No Dougal, do come in. We have a special visitor. Someone, I'm sure you'll want to see."

Dougal shut the sitting room door slowly just as Norma turned around. His face paled and then suffused with the redness of embarrassment. He came over to where Catherine was sitting and put his arm protectively on the back of her chair, squeezing her shoulder so tightly she winced.

"Well, well. Never expected to see the prodigal daughter in our home. How've you been Norma? Conquered the world yet? Why've you come to bother us now, when you stayed away all these years?"

Dougal's hostility shocked Norma. She stepped away from him, raising her hands to her face as if to protect herself. Why was he so angry? After all, it was her who had been hurt. He had done the dirty on her not the other way around.

"I was invited by my sister to your twenty-fifth wedding anniversary. No one was more surprised than me, I can tell you. Why would I want to celebrate the day on which you both stuck a knife in my heart? I think I'll go now. This was a mistake."

"No don't go Norma." Catherine glared at her husband and placed a reassuring hand on Norma's arm. "Go make us some tea Dougal and put out the scones you made this morning." Dougal went to protest then thought better of it and turned on his heel slamming the door behind him. "He'll be alright in a minute. I think he was just shocked to see you. He's become very domesticated since I was ill. We cope fine."

There was something about Catherine's tone that made Norma think they did not 'cope fine'. There was a certain bitterness in its timbre, and as Catherine looked over towards the window, Norma could see the beginning of a tear. Norma waited for Catherine to elaborate, but there was nothing forthcoming. In the ensuing silence, Norma thought about Dougal. He was still handsome although there was grey in his black curly hair. He had kept his lithe body; he was always good at sport and had obviously kept it up. But the carefree, cheerful young man he was had been replaced with an angry, tense man. In the past, he'd always been popular and sociable, up for anything, but something had changed. Norma didn't think it was only to do with her sister's illness. This change had taken place over a much longer time, she guessed. The silence was broken by Dougal returning to the room with a tea tray which he placed on the coffee table in the centre of the room.

"Why don't you pour the tea, Dougal? I'm sure Norma is parched by now." Dougal made an elaborate show of clanking the cups onto the saucers followed by the teaspoons. He lifted the teapot and began to pour.

"Would you like sugar, Norma?" he asked. "Or are you sweet enough." The sickly smile he gave her was a challenge, she knew that, but she was not going to rise to it.

"No thank you Dougal. I know it's been a long time, but you should remember I don't take sugar." As he handed her the cup, he made a point of slopping the tea in the saucer.

"Oh, sorry Norma, shall I get you a serviette?"

Catherine seemed to shrink inside herself. Her shoulders hunched, and she looked down at her hands focussing on her cup and saucer. Her face was drawn and her eyes pleading. This man was cruel. He was determined to upset their reunion. He almost threw Catherine her cup, while focussing on Norma. He didn't love her sister. Had he married her to spite Norma? She couldn't see what she had ever seen in this man apart from his *joie de vivre* and ravishing looks. He had been ambitious and all they had talked about was getting away from the islands into the big wide world. But only she had done it. But that was no reason to make her sister very unhappy, but what could she do now. It was too late. Alright, she and her sister hadn't always seen eye to eye when they were growing up, but they had always stuck up for each other and listened to each other's woes. That is until Dougal muddied the waters.

"I'll be going now Catherine," she said putting down her cup and gathering up her handbag and scarf. "I'll see you later at the party."

"Don't go yet, Norma, it's still early and we haven't really talked." Catherine's eyes were pleading but Norma was adamant. She had spent enough time here.

She kissed her sister, hugged her and got up to leave.

"Going, already are you? Will we see you in another twenty years then?" Dougal was grinning, as he led her to the front door. "Don't hurry back," he hissed. "We don't want you here."

"I bet you don't. If you hurt my sister anymore, you'll have me to answer to. What's her name? I know you didn't go to Tobermory for balloons whatever you say. Always on your way when things get difficult.' Dougal slammed the door behind her. Norma had made her decision.

195

Back in her room, she began to pack her bag. When she was ready, she knocked on Mrs Henderson's door.

"How much do I owe you? I'm not staying, I'll pay you for tonight of course."

"Are you not going to the party then?" Mrs Henderson was all ears. How did she know about the party Norma mused, then realised that in such a small place nothing was a secret?

"No something's come up. I need to leave on tonight's ferry." She knew Mrs Henderson expected more, but she was not going to get it.

After she had settled with Mrs Henderson, she loaded her bag in the car and started the engine. She had phoned ahead to make her booking, grateful that it was not peak tourist season.

At the quay she parked up and took one last look at the island. She did not belong here anymore. Let her sister and brother-in-law celebrate their twenty-five years of living a lie. She would drink to them tonight, when she was safely ensconced in a comfortable hotel room en route to her home in Manchester. She wanted no part of it. As she drove onto the ferry, she had no regrets. Dougal had come between them again.

About the author
Elizabeth lives on Anglesey. She spends her time working at the 'day job' and writing short stories, poetry and attempting to finish her first novel. She has now been published in four Bridge House anthologies: *Baubles*, *Glit-er-ary*, *Crackers* and *Nativity*. When inspiration dries up, she talks to her dog and gazes out onto her lovely garden.

"There's Rosemary, That's for Remembrance."

Linda Flynn

Doctor Archibald Tobias was found at noon, lying as still as a tomb.

There are gossips in every village and Lydney was no exception. Some claimed that mandrake roots had been boiled in his stew, a few loudly proclaimed it was witchcraft, but the softer whispers said that he had sampled some of his own medicine.

He had considered himself to be a master of his profession, trained by the best medical men in the country, at Cambridge University. His expertise earned him the right to visit the wealthiest patients around Gloucestershire, where he would bowl up in his new pony and gig. Many a wealthy land owner would sigh with relief, to see him strut through their gate with his chest out and his leather bag bulging with the latest learning. He would leave only a bill of his charges behind, with perhaps a jar of leeches for blood-letting and instructions to be presented to the apothecary for their medicines.

Whilst on his rounds he would often notice Rosemary, the village wise-woman, wending her way from one hovel to another, administering her home-spun, primitive herbal cures and he would smile.

She never returned his greetings, just narrowed her cat-like green eyes, and with a twist of her tawny head would slip off into the woodland. He noted that she seemed to glide through nature without disturbing it. Even the birds and deer did not seem to take off in flight. This was an uncommon woman.

He thought again of the haughty way she held herself upright and her disdainful gaze, as though she was the one who was high born, and found himself bristling. He whipped his pony harder than he intended, so with an abrupt wrench his trap jerked forward and he clung to the sides to steady himself.

Rosemary weaved her way through the brooding willows that found themselves alongside the meandering river, skirting its dark green glass edges, before it opened up into fields swathed with sunlit grass.

She had prepared a potion laced with a little belladonna to help with Mary's birth pains and her baby's passage into the world. Then she used a mixture of lavender and mandragora to help with John's death pains, the sleep assisting his passage into the next world.

She ambled to the village, gathering herbs in her basket, ready to give to Bess to dry out later in her cottage. They would be pummelled into potions and ointments.

As she approached the grey stone cross, where three mud tracks converged, she felt a sense of trepidation. Shadows were flung across the monument from the sprawled branches of the old oak, which were flailing in all directions. Shrill cries and raucous shouts resounded, shaking the air. She ran forward, raising her arms, as her hair slipped around her like fire. The gathering groups parted to allow her through.

In the centre of the mounted stone blocks she observed Ann, with her face flushed and her chin raised. On either side of her, with legs parted were Joshua and Tom, glaring at each other.

Rosemary nodded. She knew this pot had been about to boil.

First she beckoned Tom towards her. With defiant eyes he stepped forward. As she walked with him away from the others, she placed her arm over his. "Tom, you are to leave at daybreak, without a word to anyone. Follow the river's path westward and take yourself into one of the nearby villages. Only return when the sun has set over the river nine times, and not before. Then and only then, you should meet Ann by the Mill Bridge and present her with the most beautiful stone that you find on your travels."

To Joshua she smiled and said, "Ann is like that oak tree; her roots grow deep, solid and unmoving. You are more like the rushing brook beneath, ever restless, never still. Take your trade eastward in the direction of this river and do not return until the moon has waxed and waned a full nine times. When it has done so, you will have found the brightest sun and Ann will be but a shadow."

Rosemary ignored Ann's mutinous face as she walked her away from the on-lookers. She simply pointed to the sky and said, "Tonight look to the stars winking in the sky. Tom is your bright and constant North Star, giving you direction.

"Joshua is but a shooting star in August, shining all the more brightly for burning himself out."

Tobias watched her body wind its way through a field of wheat in a silent, smooth, sinuous movement. He noticed the way that the coarse fabric of her dress clung to her soft, white body, whilst her hair blazed out behind her in a wild, wanton display.

He saw her pause, tilting her head slightly, as a deer does when it scents danger.

As swift as the breeze she slipped off in a different direction, leaving only the nodding corn sheaves behind her.

There it came again, that pulsing heat, the sense of being observed. She scanned the clumps of trees with her sharp green eyes.

199

A snap of a twig and a rustling of wings drew her to a dark hunched shape flattened to a tree trunk.

It was not far to the farm cottage from the field, but she still had to traverse the stream that ran through the copse. Her shallow breathing caught in her throat. To break free, she would either need to go closer and then run; or she could flee in the opposite direction.

In a heartbeat she swung around and cut diagonally across the corn, feeling the blades scrape her legs. She would not turn around.

Tobias' cheeks burned. He had been turned away from the Great House; they no longer required his ministrations.

His eyes bulged as he stared into the serving girl's sparrow-like face. Old George's fever had worsened in the night, in spite of all of his blood-letting.

By morning they had brought in Rosemary with her basket of herbs, who had undone all of his good work by removing the leeches, throwing open the shutters and banking the fire.

They had chosen superstitious folklore over his wealth of learning from the most erudite men in the country.

After the Great House, Rosemary rushed to the farmhouse where she administered a blend of sage, lavender and marjoram along Nan's brow to ease her headache.

She gave some rosemary for her stomach pains and burnt the rest to clear the air. She patted Nan's hand, "Pay no heed to scandalmongers, for they have no more substance than if you look at your visage in the river, where ripples distort your image."

Tobias noticed that whilst Rosemary did not charge for her dispensations, she did not go short. For even though her cottage lay on the outskirts of the village, every day fresh goods were left on the step. He shook his head at the eggs, milk and a bolt of cloth waiting to be brought inside. Her needs were always met.

Inside Bess was drying herbs across the rafters, preparing lotions, grinding up plants and boiling potions in a rounded iron pot.

He had two assistants of his own now, scavenged from Cambridge: wiry young labourers with crooked smiles, eager to earn some money. As Rosemary appeared, hastening towards her home, he pressed a coin into each of their clammy hands. With alacrity they rushed to block her path, ogling her as they did so.

Rosemary did not halt her pace, keeping her strides long and purposeful. As she drew level she said, "The wind makes a cruel and fickle task master. It blusters and moans with a great show of strength as it fells the mighty elm."

Her dark green eyes looked straight into their faces, "But it can quickly change direction."

They stepped aside.

Often in the dark of the moon, when Rosemary lit a tallow with its flickering flame distorting shadows around her cottage, she would get a sense of a brooding ill-boding outside. Amidst the bats flitting and the swoop of a barn owl, she would see the bushes shudder, or the gate swing open, or a dark mound lying on the ground that had not been there before.

In the pool of pulsing light, she would lie on her straw pallet, listening to the foxes barking, tense and alert for any strange sounds.

Tobias stood behind the hay rick watching her water divining. The farmer wanted to know the source of the underground spring. She stood with a hazel twig in each hand, walking backwards and forwards, an absent expression on her face. Suddenly the twigs turned in towards each other and she stood motionless as the farmer pointed towards the spot.

Only the devil could be part of such sorcery.

Hunched inside Martha's hovel, she observed her weary movements. "I have prepared a chamomile tincture to help with your malady of the mind," Rosemary offered, as she crouched opposite, so that their knees were nearly touching.

"We must follow the course of the river, wherever it takes us, for that is our fate. Sometimes it twists and winds with firm, steep banks through sunny, open pastures, or clear bubbling brooks. But it also becomes deep, dark and dank, where the water hardly seems to flow. Remember that these are the places where the biggest fish grow."

She touched Martha's arm and left the ointment.

The air became stifling and still; Rosemary struggled to breathe. Her legs felt heavy as she stumbled towards her cottage. "Bess! I must take my leave, you must go!"

"No! Why?" Bess covered her face with her hands.

Rosemary slid some of her tools in a shelf up the chimney. The herbs and potions she pushed into a roof cavity. "Three witnesses claim that they saw me casting love spells by the stone cross. I am also going to be charged with practising sorcery amongst nature, locating hidden stones with mystical qualities and dispensing magical potions in Lydney village."

Bess recalled the day in her childhood when she had been forced to watch the ducking and drowning of a witch in the deepest part of the river. Her eyes widened in horror.

Rosemary led her to the door frame and as she passed through the threshold bestowed upon Bess a stealth blessing to help her remain unobserved:

"Be as still as the waiting heron,
As silent as the owl in flight,
As watchful as the eagle's eye,
And hidden in the darkest night."

Rosemary's body was hanged from the great oak tree and left there for the carrion to feed upon. On the night of a full moon it was cut down and burned. The blackened remains crumbled into the scarred, scorched earth.

Summoned to Doctor Archibald Tobias' white washed room, Bess clenched and unclenched her skirts. His face was clammy and as white as marble, as vice-like cramps clenched his stomach.

"If the doctor from the next parish cannot help you, with his bad blood-letting, then I don't know what I can do. My mistress died before I had time to learn her craft."

His pale eyes darted around the room. "What is that which lies on my window sill?" he rasped.

Bess slid over and presented the dark green stalk with purple heart-shaped petals. "It is nought but a stem of rosemary."

By noon, Doctor Archibald Tobias was found dead, crushing a sprig of rosemary between his fingers.

About the author
Linda Flynn has had two humorous novels published: *Hate at First Bite* for 7–9-year-olds and *My Dad's a Drag*, for teenagers. Both won Best First Chapter in The Writers' Billboard competition. Her children's book, *A Most Amazing Zoo* has just been released by Chapeltown Books.

She has six educational books with the Heinemann Fiction Project. In addition she has written for a number of newspapers and magazines, including theatre reviews and several articles on dogs.

Linda has had twenty short stories published for adults, children and teenagers.

Linda's website is: www.lindaflynn.com

Those Nice Suits

Hannah Retallick

It was the only time he had caught me looking. He smiled and said hello. I wasn't prepared.

Sometimes we both took the 07:51 from St Erth to London Paddington. I was always early. As pathetic as this sounds, waiting at the station with him was one of the highlights of my week. We would sit on the bench to the far right of the station, knowing, unlike some tourists and less-experienced locals, which end of the train we needed. He was always early too. A member of staff in an orange hi-vis jacket paraded the platform as it began to fill, seemingly getting a kick out of telling people the rough location of Coach J.

One of the first things I had noticed about him was that he didn't wear a watch. I know that sounds crazy but hear me out. It seems to be a 'thing' in high-flying circles, to wear the most ostentatious, expensive watch imaginable, regularly releasing it from a shirt sleeve and frowning at its ostentatious, expensive face. It annoys me, because said person has usually been staring at a screen up to that point, a screen that displays the time clearly. But no, it must be the watch – look at me, look at me, I'm running out of time, I'm important, I'm busy, busy and important, my time costs more than yours etc. Anyway, there was none of it with this guy at the station.

I dubbed him Grey Suit. Unless the weather required a black raincoat, the grey suit was all I saw him in. Grey suit with shiny black shoes. I can't say I've ever been attracted to smart business types – I know too many of them – but this guy wore it well, by which I mean he didn't seem to place importance on it. He leant back on the bench without consideration of the potential splinters or residue of rain drops and crossed his arms without fearing sleeve-creasing.

Grey Suit had a pretty face; dark, smooth skin, and a neatly trimmed black beard. Nice ears. I like nice ears. He wore bright, jewel-toned ties – red, green, or blue – a flash of life against his white shirt, always worn loosely at that stage of the morning. Not very tall. Neat figure. Arms that were not strangers to the gym but neither did they live there.

It was not his looks that grabbed me the most, before you accuse me of shallow objectification; it was his manner. Even with my sneaky glances and peripheral scanning, I could tell he was a nice person. He wasn't choosy with his eye contact. His eyes were eager to catch other people's and share positivity, chatting to anyone who was up for it, from cleaners to stuffy businessmen to lads with glazed eyes. He would have talked to me regularly, I'm sure, if I'd enabled him to break into my bubble.

I wore headphones. I listened to books on Audible or listened to music. I wanted to soften the station sounds, using the headphones as a barrier in the same way some people wear sunglasses, to shut out the whole world as well as the sun. Sometimes I wore sunglasses too.

Even though I always wanted to speak to Grey Suit, I was afraid to. I try not to discriminate, but... he was far too pretty. Talking to pretty is a struggle. I knew my words would have tumbled out in the wrong order and it would've ruined the joy of sitting next to him. My best friend, Lucy, says I'll become more confident as the years go by. She's four years older than me and takes on a grandmotherly role, emboldened by leaving me in the previous decade. Maybe when my thirties hit, I'll become an adult who can talk to guys. I doubt it though. I'm terminally pathetic.

A few years ago, Lucy and I were going on a shopping trip to the big city. Arriving at St Erth in the early morning without having eaten any breakfast, we popped into the tiny station café. The walls are covered with nostalgic Cornish memorabilia. There are three small tables and you can wreak havoc if you like to shove your chair back with no warning. It was full that day. We went up to the counter, cluttered snacks squeezed into baskets – chocolate bars, crisps, biscuits, fruit, cream crackers, all marked with handwritten labels on fluorescent cardboard stars.

"Two lattes and two bacon baps, please," I said to the lad, through the serving hatch.

"Good choice," he said, smiling. "Can't beat a bacon bap."

I smiled back. He had nice eyes, big and brown, and light red hair. Pretty. A little scruffy.

"Nice weather," he said, tapping on the counter in the little kitchen, waiting for the chug of the coffee machine.

"Yeah."

Lucy was quiet behind me. Unusually quiet.

"Where you headed?" he asked, handing us the takeout cups.

"London," I said.

"Cool."

He flipped the bacon on a little grill and chucked it onto the bread, spread with a thick layer of margarine.

"That guy liked you," Lucy observed, when we stepped outside, holding the big baps together with flimsy napkins.

"No, he didn't."

"He totally did. Couldn't stop smiling at you. Plus, we never get that many rashers normally."

"Rashers? Sounds yucky when you say it like that."

"Haha."

We finished our food, chucked the napkins in a bin, and I brushed flour off my hands.

"Do you think I should talk to him then?" I asked.

"Yes. Do it. Buy a snack."

I marched back in before I could talk myself out of it and leant on the counter with its bunting-patterned cloth. My heart thumped. His smile returned. "Hello again, how can I help you?"

"I need… chocolate."

Blur of colour. I grabbed a bar at random.

"My girlfriend loves Snickers," he said. "Can't say I'm keen. Peanuts. They make me queasy."

So, that was that. I'd been rejected without saying anything. Queasy without even eating the Snicker bar.

When I told Lucy, face burning, she said, "Never mind."

Never mind? You see, it didn't matter to her; Café Guy was just an option, someone to shrug off while looking for the next one. It was practice. She praised me for trying and I thanked her for making me do it and said she was right, it was good practice, murmuring the words into the lid of my coffee so that she wouldn't detect the fib. That tiny incident crushed me.

The day that Grey Suit finally caught me looking, all I had to do was say hello back. That's how it works, isn't it? 'Hello' turns to 'nice weather' to 'where are you headed' to 'London' to 'me too' to 'my name's Anna' to 'my name's what-ever-it-is' – from stranger to potential within a few neat sentences, his interest locking onto yours until you're both at risk of missing the train. I didn't say hello back though; I didn't remove my headphones; and I didn't manage more than a mild smile. Terminally pathetic.

If I'd known I wouldn't see him again, perhaps it would have been different – perhaps I would have been different. I often picture him on a different train, an earlier one, or a later one, due to a shift in his working patterns, a promotion that he deserves because he's so conscientious and there is no one better when it comes to people management. I'm happy for him.

The station has become lonely for me. It never was before. I look up more these days, often leaving my book in my bag, studying everyone as they trundle by with battered suitcases. There are plenty of people around, all bleary and automatic, but they don't catch my eye, none of them do. Grey Suit would have.

It's a Monday morning in May. Warm and breezy. Quiet platform. I put in my headphones and continue to listen to a self-help book. I wonder if I should stop with the whole winning friends and influencing people thing and instead choose something with a title like *How to Get a Grip and Stop Being Pathetic*. There's a book that's dying to be written. I close my eyes.

A moment later, I feel a movement. A navy suit perches on the edge of my bench, trying not to be intrusive, staring at his phone. He switches from Messenger to email, over and over, even though nothing new comes through. Suddenly becoming conscious of me, he moves his hand so that the screen isn't visible. He taps his brown-shod feet and glances left and right, as though waiting to cross a busy road.

Navy Suit has a gentler appearance than Grey Suit – soft light brown hair and a face that doesn't look like it could be easily frustrated despite the relentless fidgeting. Calm face in a twitchy body. Active. Strong in other people's crises and anxious in his own. Reckon he's nice, sweet, kind. Understanding. He has eyes that would be nice to catch, if I could.

I can mull it over as much as I like, and find ways to justify my consistent inaction, but the truth is, I've simply grown used to making myself invisible. It's easier. It's comfortable. Imaginary romances have a certain amount of

209

charm. I can't do it forever though. I can't spend my whole life glancing at lovely strangers without talking to them.

The train rumbles towards the station. I quickly remove my headphones.

"Hello," I say, as we both stand, my heart kicking my ribs. He looks my way, pauses, and manages a mild smile.

That's it. We climb onto the train and head into opposite carriages. I take an aisle seat, placing my khaki backpack on the window seat; that generally keeps people away until I'm forced to give it up when the train fills later in the journey. I draw my laptop from my bag to do some work ahead of an afternoon of meetings.

My thoughts drift to Navy Suit. A mild smile. I'd taken him by surprise, tried to start a conversation at a silly moment. If I see him again, I'll say hello immediately, right as he sits down, and invite him to shuffle closer – or at least have both buttocks on the bench! That would break the ice. Navy Suit will say hello back next time; I'm certain of that. He'll be more prepared. I might still mess the whole thing up, jabbering on and showing too much of my weirdness in one go, but what does that really matter? At least it would only be momentarily pathetic. I refuse to be terminal.

About the author

Hannah Retallick is a twenty-six-year-old from Anglesey, North Wales. She was home-educated and then studied Creative Writing with the Open University. She was shortlisted in the Writing Awards at the Scottish Mental Health Arts Festival 2019, the Cambridge Short Story Prize, the Henshaw Short Story Competition June 2019, and the Bedford International Writing Competition.

https://ihaveanideablog.wordpress.com/

Twelve Black:

Christopher Bowles

There are a lot of stories about witches.

In some, they are wrinkled old hags that bathe in the blood of virgins in order to restore lost youth and beauty. In others, they enchant apples with enticing poisons, begging for supple throats in which to stick like pins. Most depict them as hideous crones with green skin and tell-tale warts. They're capable of turning men into pigs, and building candy-cane houses to ensnare wayward children. They seduce young men, corrupt female protégés, and kidnap the young and naive to raise as their own.

They have mastery over the elements, boiling the humours of the body, and summoning fires from the circles of Hell. They call forth raging winds, natural disasters – earthquakes, plagues, famines and war. They turn into dragons, wolves, panthers and ravens. They have eyes in every shadow. Skulls on every windowsill. Spells for every occasion.

Some say they are in league with the Devil – that they sold their souls for a taste of his secret arts. Some say they were once apothecaries, intoxicated by lethal herbs and poultices to the point of no return. Some say they are simply malicious ghouls, with solid jet black eyes and razor-edged teeth.

As for myself? Well… I don't know what to believe. At times, I dismiss it all as fancy. Mere fabrication. Monstrous villains dreamt up by parents to keep their misbehaving children in check. What are these supposed witches, if not merely women? Desperate women with desires and needs.

Surely they are no more dangerous than any other woman, scorned or not?

But there are other times, when my voice of reason is quietened. When my wife has retired for the evening. When I'm alone at night, watching the fireplace with a certain anxiety. When I think of how the other villagers look at me oddly; when they call me heretic under their breath and question why I allow my love to be as forthright and domineering as any man. When they question our equality.

When I hear whispers at my back, and shudder, as someone, somewhere tiptoes 'cross my grave. It is in these quiet moments of solace, that I begin to fear. That I begin to doubt what little I can half-invoke.

That I begin to think, and remember...

I can't recall the names. Only the faces. And even then, sometimes I fear that might be too much. How often I have tried to forget. To seal tight these pictures and words as if in a dream, forgotten when I wake. But yet, how often have I tried to recall them. For clarity's sake. To ease my conscience. To sleep soundly.

It was many years ago.

I was in my prime back then; not yet thirty. I had travelled from town to town, yearning to experience the lives of others, still seeking my trade. I had become a jack-of-all-trades, mostly labouring in each new village; still to find my calling. I envied the towns where everyone knew their place, where professions had been allotted at birth, and were simply titles, not based on skill or aptitude. I came from a line of medics myself, but in each new stop on my journey, the position of town doctor was fiercely guarded by their own bloodline. It didn't matter how well I could name the bones of the human body, or draw and label the inner workings of the heart or brain or lungs. I was always just a spare part.

So after nearly ten years of wandering, I eventually settled -for nearly three years, in fact – in a quiet hamlet off the Southern coast. The town physician was getting old, and had no heirs; and took my appearance as a sign from God. He welcomed me as an apprentice; and took me into his home as his tutelage of me began to pay off. After two years under his wing, the old man died – not peacefully in his sleep as expected, but after being struck by a cart in the road. The townsfolk were all too eager to welcome me as his successor; and so for a further year I remained, having finally found a home, a job, and a community who respected me.

There couldn't have been many more than three hundred souls in the place. Everyone knew each other by name, by occupation, by secret. Illicit affairs were conducted behind closed doors, but widely spoken of. Under the wing of the village doctor, diseases were diagnosed that the neighbours already knew about. Not a birth, not a death, not a sneeze was conducted without the knowledge of the whole town. They were practicing masters of turning the blind eye. Veterans of the open secret. And so I became a part of them, learning their ways, their secrets, and their manner.

It was however, one summer that they came. The women.

The oldest man in the village – a retired cobbler – had died three weeks prior, and it was my first time to pronounce a death without the guidance of my now dead senior. They came to claim his belongings, and we presumed, to clean up and sell his house. For such a close-knit community, as a group we were surprised to find he had any family left. But sure enough, they came; arriving under the cover of night. And as the dawn broke, signalling the start of his funereal proceedings, we saw them all for the very first time.

A woman, old and bent like a curved stalk of wheat. She spiralled over and into herself, and had a face that puckered and soured like a rotting grape. She seemed menial enough, for an old woman. Voice like a hacksaw, yet smiled kindly through sparsely rooted teeth and rotted gums. She was the Matriarch; had she the years or energy left, she would have run the household.

But instead, it was her daughter who took up the reins. The Mother. She was willowy. Fragile-looking, with wispy hair and a perpetual look of distance in her face. She in turn, had three daughters, all of whom shared an ethereal sense of something about them. Cloudy hair gathering about their faces like smoke or tufts of wool, but each having distinctly different faces. The eldest was harsh, pinched and sour. The middle child was the opposite, rounded and jovial. And the youngest was pretty. Baby-faced like a cherub and sweet.

The sixth member of the household was the Maiden. No-one dared ask her relation to the other two adults, but it was clear she was not a sister to the three other younglings in the house. Her skin was tinged with olive; and her eyes fiery. She always sported an elaborate head-wrap, hiding whatever hair she may have had. She also had a baby. A mewling, squawking infant girl.

A house of seven women, and not a man to be seen. It was bound to invite trouble.

And so trouble came.

After the funeral, we expected them to put the house in order, and then to leave. We never even thought they'd opt to stay. But apparently, the house was much more than they currently had – a luxury of more rooms than mouths to feed, all under one roof.

I used to watch them from time to time. The old man's house was in the centre of town, and therefore, so were they. They were crowbarred into the heart of a closed community. Injected like a virus. And it was not taken politely. They were eschewed. Confined to the outskirts of this enclosed society, yet strangely at the core of it. Treated like lepers if they weren't outright avoided or ignored. They never begged. Never stole. They bought their food wordlessly and retreated back into the haven of the crooked house. And they were content to live this way. In more luxury than had ever been afforded them, but at the cost of all social contact with the outside world. It was a peaceful, if not precarious arrangement. And one that would inevitably come crashing to a close.

It started at the fringes first. The elderly women of the commune started gossiping more often; their words becoming more vicious and serrated than usual. Not just about the women in the crooked house, but about their neighbours, their friends, their acquaintances.

Arguments across the village began to crop up more frequently. From my windowsill, it was almost like I could see the atmosphere change. I could imagine a dark cloud descending on the rooftops, trickling down the chimneys and seeping under the cracks in the door. The very fabric of the community had been tainted, and was slowly succumbing to an unknown corruption.

It emerged, in the dying days of August, that the middle daughter had been dallying with the baker's son. There was a spectacle. Public shouting. His father beat him and belted him, and made him sleep on the porch for three days until he promised never to see her again. She never left the house once during this time.

Then, come autumn, the butcher and his wife had a public spat. He accused her of sleeping with his much younger brother who had been staying with them for the past year. It turned ugly. Physical. The two brothers fought in the street, whilst she wailed from the side-lines, and there was a sudden blow. A glancing fist. An unlucky angle. And the butcher dropped down dead, bleeding all over the cobblestones.

It was deemed an accident, and when the trial took place, the jury were succinct. There had to be a unanimous vote, in order to pass any sentence, or alleviate any crime, and all twelve jurors were content to claim the brother's innocence.

The butcher's wife, however, was inconsolable, affronted as her guilt was implicated. And she was made homeless as the business and entire estate were passed down to his brother, who promptly took out his guilt and grief on her. To the surprise of everyone in the town, she sought refuge with the vagabonds. The gypsies. The unfortunates. She knocked on the door of the wisp-women. The ladies with the cloudy hair and smoky eyes, and they invited her in without complaint.

The house of seven was now a house of eight.

When tongues began wagging, and rumours started to wing about the hamlet like tiny sparrows in flight, the butcher's brother began to grow angry. He accused the household of attempting to poison the village against him. His tirade was long and arduous, and for nearly a week, every waking hour of the day he would stand outside their door, shouting until his voice was rough and hoarse; claiming witchcraft! Demon! Harlot!

"Something in that house had poisoned her!" he would cry. "Her mind is not her own!"

Even though he had denounced her affections, and publicly shamed her, it would appear to not be enough to sate his destructive appetites. He wanted to hound her from the town, to remove all bloodied traces of his brother from his hands. And yet she was harboured, in the centre of town. By social pariahs.

A similar fate befell several other inhabitants. The constant arguing across the rooftops came to a crux, and one day two women had finally had enough. They left their husbands – one of whom had a young slip of a girl in tow – and packed their bags. Without speaking, both wives found themselves at the doorstep of the crooked house in the centre of town; and the house of eight became a house of eleven.

The following week, the back-breaking straw was dealt. Although we never saw the moment it happened – tongues wagged that it must have happened in the witching hours – but one morning we saw the pastor's wife leaving the crooked house with the two wives. Arm in arm, they left the village to pick wildflowers, and on their return they all re-entered the same house with the warped roof.

It spread like wildfire – even the church was not spared from this stain. Of course, the townsfolk demanded answers; clamouring at the door of the pastor's church-side cottage. When he eventually answered, he was drunk; belligerent when shouts and wails were thrown at him.

The only house that seemed to go on as normal was a house of twelve women. I watched the shadows of their evening meal from my window.

They seemed happy.

And throughout this raging, no-one noticed the cattle, as they grew sick and thin and pale. And nobody noticed how they gradually gave out less and less milk. It wasn't until only blood and pus could be wrung from their udders that we realised a plague of sorts had befallen the livestock, and they had to be rounded up, lead away, slaughtered and burnt on the mountainside three miles out of town.

A call to arms.

The village rallied behind his accusations, men and women and children alike. "Witch!" They cried. "Witch!"

"Witch! Witch! Witch!"

A guard was set up around the house of the wisp-women. Men armed with pitchforks and scythes, children with sickles and housewives bearing blazing torches. And they watched. And waited.

The village council; three men of differing generations – an elderly man who looked like the bark of a great oak, the middle-aged blacksmith, ruddied and constantly soiled from the forge; and a fair-haired youth from the flour-mill – gathered and a ballot was drawn. Names were read out on tiny scrolls of paper, the tenth of which bore mine. The jury had been decided, the lines of war had been drawn, and the wisp-women were about to face trial.

In the library of the town hall, we faced each other. Gathered amongst the histories and bound legends, underneath the watchful eyes of the twin statues of Mercy and Justice. Twelve souls – six men and six women, all randomly selected, and yet all startlingly distinct.

Two fathers – the younger a field-labourer barely a day over twenty-one, and the elder, father to two grown women, and grandfather of five.

The local fisherman, honest and trustworthy; and the widower who sang the rites for the dead whenever we held a funeral.

A married couple whom had birthed a stillborn child the year before I arrived in the village.

Three women from the same circle of friends – two of whom were gossips who looked down on the third, a mother of three constantly squalling boys.

And finally, one of the old matrons of the village – a fierce old woman with a sharp tongue; and a young orphan girl of about nineteen, who worked as a barmaid in the tavern.

And so we heard the evidence, and the Hall was packed to the rafters. Whoever could not attend ensured the wisp-women remained sanctioned within their homely prison, and added another torch or blade to the ring of sentries.

We heard from the baker how they had tried to seduce his son. How they tried to corrupt his household from within. And I could not help but condemn him for his ridiculousness. Clutching at straws. As if he himself had never tried to steal away with a young and forbidden love?

We heard from the butcher's brother, how the witches had poisoned his lover against him, and turned him against his own flesh and blood, resulting in the death of one, and the assimilation of the other. We heard his hateful rages. His imaginative theories and outlandish claims. How he dared to suggest that his former lover may have in fact, been a witch all along...

We heard from the two disgruntled husbands – one of whom had clearly been drinking heavily, slurring his words and making little sense even at his most lucid. The other, the one with the daughter was inconsolable; mostly crying and only offering despondent broken phrases.

The priest gave his most impassioned sermon; condemning the women in the crooked house as unholy and sacrilegious.

Then we heard from the cattle-herd. Trusted, a long time server of the village needs. How he had, in his years, never seen or heard of a disease quite like the one that so brutally and efficiently devoured his livelihood. We saw a broken, desperate man laying blame on a circled target.

No-one but myself, it seemed, paused to question that we were judging a house of twelve women based on the testimony of six men. And under the watchful eye of three male councillors – who acted as judges. I guess nothing else could be expected from a town where only men had positions of power.

Afterwards, we adjourned, and argued relentlessly into the night. The two fathers, both young and old and the childless mother were adamant in the household's guilt. The gossips too, both were swayed by the persuasions of those with children to protect, and glared angrily when their friend refused stubbornly to follow suit. The rest of us clung to what we could see so plainly – the unfortunate events that had happened around the arrival of the wisp-women were distinctly separate from the accused women. They were merely fortuitous scapegoats. Women who had over-extended their generosity and were doomed to pay the price.

The matron and the orphan were the strongest voices of reason alongside my own. The widowed singer too, began to grow with confidence as his voice was muffled, eventually bellowing out to be heard. The childless father, turned against his wife, was a particularly difficult moment to witness. The fisherman, and the gossips' friend bringing up the rear, but by no means out of the debate.

It grew heated. We paused, ate, reconvened. And it looked like we would never see eye to eye. And yet, we knew. Every one of us. That we would have to reach a unanimous decision in order to pass any form of verdict. It had been difficult for others before us, and it would no doubt be difficult now. But we knew some of us would have to turn our backs on our own beliefs. Our own convictions.

And how would we live with ourselves?

We cast our stones – white for innocent, black for guilty, into the leather bag. This was presented to the council, who revealed the contents. Five black, seven white.

That night I dreamt fitfully. I remembered my sister; who was so much more suited for medicine than I. She took to autopsy like a duck to water. I remembered how she performed imaginary surgeries on her dolls; how she helped me learn rhymes to name all the bones in the human arm and hand. How she never flinched at the sight of blood.

I woke wishing that that she were in my place.

The next day, we set aside our daily chores and issues to meet once more in the library. Beneath Mercy and Justice we argued, and still the votes remained the same. Another split vote. The council dismissed us once more.

I don't remember what I dreamt of that second night, but I do recall rising with the bed sheets stuck to me, drenched in sweat and smelling of fear.

On the third day, however, there was a sudden and alarming change of heart. Only myself, the orphaned girl and the childless father remained to fight for their innocence. The singer was the first to cave, seemingly swayed by the honeyed words of the young father. Then the old woman and the fisherman, both of whom had downcast eyes and seemingly heavier pockets. The mother of the triplet boys simply cried throughout the duration of our meeting.

Bribery, perhaps? Threats? These were morally upstanding

members of our society, and they were falling like flies to the corruption.

It was barely a surprise to me, that when the council revealed the bag of judgement before the village, that they extracted twelve polished black stones.

There was uproar.

Three – if not four of those stones should have been white, and we all knew it. Even those who had been seduced were outraged. But the voices of the jury were drowned out by the bays of the crowd.

Blood, they wanted.

Blood, they demanded.

Blood they shall have.

The pitchforks and scythes closed in.

The town hall emptied into the street; villagers had spilled out like flies. The council lead the procession to the crooked house; and shouted for calm. They lined us up – the jurors, and placed torches in our hands. We were to be the front line. The executioners.

And the elder, the great oak himself, began to read aloud. It was a long, surprisingly dreary speech; but to all those in attendance, it was what they had been waiting for. It was justice.

With my free hand, I reached for the closed fist of the orphaned barmaid beside me. Her eyes were also clenched tightly shut, tears streaming down her face. But she relaxed her fingers and took mine gratefully. At the other end of the line, I could see the mother of the triplets and the childless father struggling to compose themselves.

The door opened, and the Maiden emerged. She stood unrepentant, wild-eyed, her head-wrap fluttering wildly in a breeze that only then started to pick up. She cast a gaze across the population of the town; across the judges and the jurors whose fingers throbbed with the knowledge of palming black stones.

She tore her wrap off and cast it to the winds. Her hair flew about her shoulders in loose ribbons, and she never looked more beautiful to me. Or more dangerous. The babe in her arms began to mewl.

"If you must punish us? Do what you wish. We have seen your so-called 'Justice'. We have felt your supposed 'Mercy'. You think us witches? Then witches we must be! Come, fill me Satan! Root your evil in me and spew thy wretched seed! When the smoke clears, I dare you to find just one soul amongst you who can claim to be any less monstrous than the witches you believe we are!"

And for a moment, she met my gaze, and seemed to soften. Her eyes met the barmaid's as well, and for the briefest of seconds, I thought I saw the Maiden smile.

And with that, she soothed the baby in its swaddling, and retreated back into the house.

The council gave the order, and the jurors started the first tongues of fire; eight torches licking the crooked walls of the crooked house. The mother of triplets rushed to my side and collapsed into the crook of my arm, sobbing into my chest. I felt the orphan girl's grip tighten.

The three of us stood and watched; the only stillness as the throng closed in, and the wisp-women's house went up in flames.

There were no screams. No pleas. The door never opened.

Not even when the roof fell in, collapsing under the smoke and the weight of its burning bulk. And when the ashes were cool enough to be examined, we found, in a near perfect circle, the bones of twelve figures. Twelve blackened skulls accusingly staring back up at us from the face of a clock of death.

The orphan girl shared my bed that night; but even after the warm echo of her flesh against mine began to cool with the night air, I slept fitfully. I wandered through a dream valley lined with charred skulls. Twelve polished black stones set in the hollow left sockets of those twelve blackened skulls. The eleventh was so small I nearly missed it, and the last wore a head-wrap and glistened with malice. Twelve evil eyes.

I arose with the first sounds of dawn, nakedly stumbling to the window to look down at the still-smoking ruins of the crooked house. The orphan girl breathed deeply, unstirred behind me in the bed.

Nine bodies had been discovered during the night. The bodies of those who had condemned the wisp-women.

The young father, suspended by a thick rope and a shattered neck in the barn.

The fisherman, floating face down in the shallow waters by the docks.

The childless mother slit her wrists in the armchair downstairs. The father, driven apart by the judgement, slept in the master bedroom alone, and had barely noticed her absence.

His two daughters found the older father, choked on his own swollen tongue in the night.

The gossips were both found with the hilt of a knife in their hands, the blades buried into the heart of the other. A pact, perhaps?

Their friend, the mother, found at the foot of the stairs by her children. Back broken in three places. Head completely twisted around on her shoulders.

The old woman had had a heart attack.

And the widowed singer had simply died peacefully in his sleep. Wasted away.

How curious an incident, we all thought.

What mindless, violent acts.

The orphan girl and I. We watched the village descend into fear. Into paranoia. Into madness. We dressed, and went to pay vigil at the ruins of the crooked house. The childless father joined us, and we simply stared as the mob turned on the council. The blacksmith blamed the treachery on the young miller, and as they fought, the crowd descended on them with their hands, tearing them both apart with their fists. Rending limb from limb. The elder simply walked out to sea, past the floating corpse of the drowned fisherman, until the bubbles stopped popping on the surface of the water.

However, they never turned their angry hands upon us. It was almost as if we couldn't even be seen.

That night again, I shared a bed with the orphan girl, and dreamt of the new bodies I'd have to examine in the morning. The nine corpses of the jurors that I'd have to study and help bury; and the three councillors. I wondered how we'd handle the rites of the dead wisp-women and the villagers that had been burned with them.

And it filled me with sadness to realise that the mother of the triplets had been crying out of guilt, and that she truly had cast a black stone at the vital hour.

I awoke at midnight.

I could not explain how or why. The simplest explanation I have is that I felt beckoned. Like that same cloud that had descended on the village only a fortnight before had come calling once more.

Looking back at the bed, I saw she was gone; and I found myself unworried.

Sudden movement brought me to the window. The Maiden's head-wrap, caught on a protruding nail on the frame. I unhooked it, and clutched it in my hands calmly. From my perch, I could see the rubble of the crooked house begin to stir.

And so the call came, and I answered; dressing quickly.

The Matriarch had already pulled herself, reformed and unscarred from the ash and blackened rubble. The childless father was already at her side, dusting off her clothes with unexpected tenderness. As I approached, the Maiden rose, soot spilling from her shoulders. The babe in her arms clucked happily and tugged at her hair. She took my face in her free hand, and held it close to her own and she smiled warmly.

Her stare seemed to let everything fall into place. I realised that the Mother would not be coming back. She was simply a waif from another town, accepted into the fold alongside her daughters, as the scorned women from this town had been. The Maiden before me, with her own child... She was the real Mother.

"My daughter tells me you are a rare beast indeed. An honest man."

And I turned, knowing what I would see. The orphan girl. The true Maiden.

I offered the wrap to the Mother, and took the Maiden's hands in my own.

"Will you come?"

Of course, I accepted.

So we left the village. My new family and I. The childless father doted on the Mother in the same way that I showed obvious affection for the Maiden. His eyes lit up whenever the babe looked at him. And as we reached the top of the hill, where the wildflowers grew, I turned to look back at the hamlet. And we huddled as a group, against the cold, and warmed ourselves as the first signs of smoke started drifting from the town hall.

We watched the town burn in the dead of night.

But only for a little while.

Yes; there are a lot of stories about witches.

And they all end in blood.

And fire.

About the author
Christopher Bowles is an award-winning playwright and National Slam Champion of performance poetry. He founded Magpie Man Theatre in 2015; and recently published his first collection of flash fiction, *Spectrum*. He is a big fan of both coffee and chocolate, and accepts all donations gladly.

Waiting for the Pigeons

Tony Oswick

A car speeds down the road. For an instant, its headlights illuminate the windows like an explosion of sheet lightning. The roaring noise lives on for a moment more and then it's gone. Thunder storms, fire crackers or the constant wailing of a car alarm might wake the street. But the street sleeps on. Am I the only one to hear the car? Is the driver a late reveller or an early worker? A late reveller probably. Why would they be so eager to get to work? I console myself there's someone else awake at four o'clock in the morning.

The darkness is a blanket enveloping me. A single lamp-post outside provides a life-line to the world. Its blurred glow stains the curtains, a comforting reassurance. Two months ago, there was a power cut and the light disappeared. The blackness was complete and I was a primitive tribesman whose world had collapsed when the moon disappeared behind a cloud. I'd lost a trusted friend. Darkness so exaggerates loneliness.

When Andrew was young, we bought him a bedside-lamp because he imagined ghoulish creatures were invading his bedroom. The lamp-shade had pictures of Tigger on it. Andrew talked to Tigger for ages before he was hypnotised to sleep. The lamp's still in my spare bedroom. I tried it once, just to see if Tigger could hypnotise me, but all he did was throw up ghostly memories. I ought to give the lamp back to Andrew. Perhaps little Jake might like it? I'll ask Andrew when I see him next. Whenever that may be.

I glance at the clock. The numbers shine like unwanted beacons. 4.18 am. The day's now four hours and eighteen minutes old. That's two hundred and fifty-eight minutes, over fifteen thousand seconds. In the next sixty seconds the '18' will change to '19'. It may take a whole minute or it could be the very next second. I count to thirty-three and the '18' changes to '19'.

Why can't I sleep? Gretchen said it was because I'm a worrier, told me I could worry for England. She was the only one who understood me. Cocooned in my bed, I can't escape. Worries multiply. I want distraction, need noise. Cats caterwauling, air-craft flying low, milk floats squealing. Anything. I do miss Gretchen.

I always have the radio on. The World Service. If ever I go on Mastermind, that will be my specialist subject. 'World News 2010–2019'. In the last hour, I've heard about political crises in Syria, floods and fires in Australia and a potential ecological disaster in the Amazonian rain forest. It's verbal wallpaper but at least it diverts my mind from the things I can't forget.

4.29 am. I've dozed for six minutes. Can it really be a whole six minutes? It's my first sleep of the night. I rejoice. But why have I woken so soon?

It wasn't always like this. Robert was never the worrier of the family, even in the bleakest of times, but it was different when we were together. The presence of another person, even one as distant as Robert had become, was a comfort. I used to talk to him while he slept. "We can't go on like this. The business is going down. It's coming between us. What would you do if I left?" I wonder if he ever heard what I said? Perhaps I subconsciously wanted him to hear. When I finally told him I was leaving, he didn't seem shocked. Perhaps he knew it was coming.

The announcer on the radio is saying today's 14th February, Valentine's Day. I'd forgotten. What a depressing day, even for someone of my age. Pink hearts rub salt into my wounds. How long has it been since someone cared?

229

I shouldn't care about cards. I don't care about birthday cards any more, don't like to be reminded of the passing years. And at Christmas, people send cards out of duty – send a card, you'll get one back. But Andrew never sends me anything on Mother's Day. It may only acknowledge a biological fact but I so want to think he cares.

And on Valentine's Day? I envisage the Post Office heaving with mail, postmen encumbered with heavy sacks, sheaves of cards falling on door-mats. On everyone's except mine. You have to care, have to make an effort to send a Valentine's card. When Robert and I were together I didn't think about it. He never sent a card or bought flowers but it didn't matter. Now I'm on my own, it seems so important.

I worry about the past which I can't change and worry about the future because of the past. I don't see Robert now. I never hated him although I wouldn't blame him if he hated me. But he was weak. When the business folded, he seemed surprised. We had to sell the house. It wasn't just the material things. Not just the money. I wanted more out of life. More excitement. Less failure. Andrew and Gretchen were both teenagers. They could look after themselves and Gretchen could look after Robert. People criticised me. "How could you leave your own children?" they said. But the children were better off without me.

I stare at the ceiling but all I see is emptiness. If you stare long enough, you start seeing shapes and movements, and if you concentrate hard enough you can make things go lighter. I can see the tiniest chink of light which has escaped between the curtains. It's planted itself in the corner of the room. Just a sliver. If I opened the curtains a little, there'd be more light from the street-lamp but then I wouldn't be able to sleep because it was too light. But I can't sleep now when it's dark.

I turn to the clock. It's 4.38 am. I so want to dream again.

Gretchen was never a wild child but she enjoyed life. Wanted to do things, see things, be someone. I could understand that, she was like me. Said university was a waste of time, wanted to make her mark in the real world. Got a good job that took her all over the country, abroad as well. She loved travelling. Then I got that telephone call from Robert. I couldn't understand it, still don't.

No-one will ever persuade me she did it deliberately. Why would she want to end it all? I'll never believe that. The overdose was just a tragic accident. Experimentation gone wrong. Robert never blamed me directly but, at her funeral, I saw accusation in his eyes. Andrew said nothing, almost as though I didn't exist. I miss seeing Jake. Every child should have a loving grandmother. Gretchen would have understood.

4.45 am. Another night's coming to an end. Two more hours and the day-light will relieve me of my burden. Why are things never quite so bad in the day time? Two more hours and I'll hear those pigeons fluttering their wings on my roof, their feet tap-tap-tapping on the guttering, waking their nearest and dearest with their constant cooing.

Two more hours. Waiting for the pigeons.

About the author
An East Londoner by birth and upbringing, Tony has lived in Clacton-on-Sea for 50 years. After a life-time of work – in the Civil Service and then the funeral service – he's now enjoying his retirement. Tony has been 'writing for pleasure' for over ten years, and is a founder-member of The Seaview Scribblers, a Clacton writing group, and Wivenhoe Shed Writers.

Index of Authors

Other Publications by Bridge House

Nativity

edited by Debz Hobbs-Wyatt and Gill James

Many of the stories in this collection take place at or near
Christmas time. There are stories of new births, of rebirths,
of new beginnings, and there are a couple that deal with the
joys and sorrows of the annual Nativity Play.

There are some familiar authors in this volume and also some
new writers. We treasure them all.

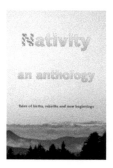

"A most unexpected collection of stories, focused on new
beginnings and rebirth. It's definitely not your traditional
nativity theme, but so much more. The stories are so varied,
dramatic, melancholic, dark and comedic, there is a story to
suit everyone." (*Amazon*)

Order from Amazon:

Paperback: ISBN 978-1-907335-76-1
eBook: ISBN 978-1-907335-77-8

Crackers

edited by Debz Hobbs-Wyatt and Gill James

Every year we pick a very vaguely Christmas-related theme
for our annual anthology. Then we invite our writers to
subvert it. In this collection, they've certainly done that to
the extent that we almost had a picture of cream crackers for
the cover. Our theme this year is "crackers". So, we have
Christmas crackers, cream crackers, cracking dresses, a
cracked antique and many, many other interpretations. We
hope you will find this a cracking good read.

"A wonderfully quirky and eccentric collection of short stories.
Each one has a different take on the notion of 'crackers' with a
heart of darkness resonating throughout. A book of little
morality gems!" (*Amazon*)

Order from www.bridgehousepublishing.co.uk

Paperback: ISBN 978-1-907335-59-4
eBook: ISBN 978-1-907335-60-0

Glit-er-ary

edited by Debz Hobbs-Wyatt and Gill James

This glittery collection of glit-er-ary tales will add some
sparkle to your life. You will meet all kinds of interesting
characters facing all kinds of interesting dilemmas.

You will learn that all that glitters is most certainly not gold.
The stories are funny, sad, poignant… the glitter comes in
shades of dark and light. But all will leave their sparkle in
your imagination.

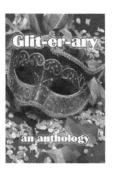

"This book is a little gem. Some beautiful writing - thoroughly
enjoyed this as something to dip in and out of for some much
needed escapism" (*Amazon*)

Order from www.bridgehousepublishing.co.uk

Paperback: ISBN 978-1-907335-55-6
eBook: ISBN 978-1-907335-56-3

Lightning Source UK Ltd.
Milton Keynes UK
UKHW022034301120
374347UK00007B/221